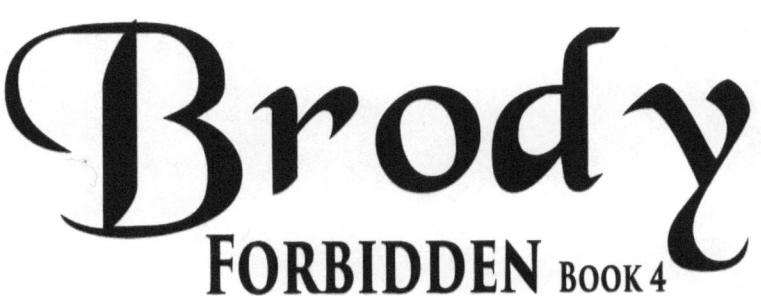

# Brody
## FORBIDDEN BOOK 4

# KATHI S. BARTON

This is a work of fiction. Names, characters, places, and incidents are products of the author's imagination or are used fictitiously and are not to be construed as real. Any resemblance to actual events, locations, organizations, or persons, living or dead, is entirely coincidental.

**World Castle Publishing, LLC**
Pensacola, Florida
Copyright © Kathi S. Barton 2019
Paperback ISBN: 9781949812671
eBook ISBN: 9781949812688
First Edition World Castle Publishing, LLC, February 4, 2019
http://www.worldcastlepublishing.com
**Licensing Notes**
Cover: Karen Fuller
Editor: Maxine Bringenberg

# Chapter 1

Brody was ready for his own bed. Well, one where a five-year-old wasn't sleeping with him. Jordan, he'd come to realize, was a bed hog. Looking over at him, Brody fell deeper in love with the little boy. He was going to be his.

On the third day of their vacation, he'd realized that Jordan had never asked about his mom. Not once did he wake in the middle of the night calling for her. And he'd never, when buying gifts for Grandma and Howie, as his butler liked to be called now, did he even suggest that he get anything for his mom. That, to Brody, was just sad. Jordan would answer questions about her when asked, mostly by strangers, but nothing about her otherwise. This was their last day, and he needed to talk to his son. Jordan, as usual, beat him to the draw. Like he knew.

"Dad, are we going home today? I sure miss my bed. And you not sleeping in it." They both laughed. "I can't wait to give my gifts to Grandma and Howie. But...Dad, will Mom be there?"

His question was quiet, like he was almost afraid to ask it. Or, Brody thought, it could have just been him *thinking* that's

5

what Jordan was doing. Sitting down at the small table they had in their room, he handed Jordan his glass of orange juice.

"No. She won't be there. But I told you, we're not going home." He nodded. "Jordan, would you be upset if she didn't come with us to the new house?"

"No." He looked at his dad, then back at his now empty glass. "She's not nice. And she yells at me all the time. She says awful things about you and Grandma. And when she has her friends over, I have to stay in the kitchen with Howie all the time."

More and more things were coming out about his wife. Rachel had made Jordan take swimming lessons, the beginner classes, so she could be in the pool with the younger mothers. Jordan was an advanced swimmer, and had hated the way his mom acted. He never got to go out to eat with her—it was drive through or nothing. And then he wasn't allowed to eat in the car. Little things, yes, but they'd mounted up heavily on the little boy.

"I'm sorry about that. I'm glad that you've told me all these things, but I'm very sorry that she treated you this way, Jordan. You believe me, don't you?" He nodded and Brody took a deep breath before speaking again. "We're getting a divorce, your mom and I. We're not going to be living together anymore."

The hopeful look in Jordan's eyes was there and gone so quickly, Brody was sure that he had mistaken it again. When Jordan started playing with his bowl of cereal, Brody decided it was time to tell him the truth about everything. But Jordan spoke before he could.

"Dad, will I have to go and live with her? I don't want to. I don't even like her." Brody didn't know what to say, so said nothing. "I know you're not my daddy. I wish you were all the time. But if you keep me and not give me to Mom, I will be the best boy in the entire world."

"Oh, Jordan." He held him tightly, tears filling his eyes even as Jordan sobbed on his chest. But what broke Brody's heart more was how Jordan kept begging him not to make him go back to his mom. Never. "You won't. I promise. And Jordan, you are a good boy. So good that I'm jealous I wasn't that good when I was small. Grandma is going to be living with us in our new place, as well as Howie."

"You promise I won't have to go to her?" He said that he did, on his life. Brody only hoped that Jake was a good enough attorney to make it happen. "I love you, Dad. Forever."

The rest of the morning was spent packing up their things. They didn't have to leave until later today, but they could take their luggage to the airport and then not have to mess with it later. They had taken two bags each, and now had four bags each. Most of it was things that Jordan wanted for his new room.

The walk around the city was nice. Brody knew that as soon as he was with Jake and the rest of his group that he'd have to settle down and get busy on this divorce. Talking to his mom nightly had helped — both he and Jordan, as a matter of fact. So he was up-to-date on things that were going on at home.

Brody knew that Rachel hadn't shown up for her court date. And he knew why. She'd been in a jail cell — for not paying her bill to the hotel — since the morning she was to appear. He had to laugh every time he thought about her being taken out in handcuffs while trying her very best to sell off some of the things in the room.

Rachel's mother, Becky Sharp, had cooperated with the police. What with her husband David being in jail too, Becky had no choice except to get out of the house nicely. And when searched, she'd not taken anything. So Brody, even though he didn't care for her husband or her daughter, paid for two weeks in a hotel for her, with food and room service included—as long as she didn't try and steal anything or harbor her daughter.

"You should have seen it, Brody. I tell you, Howie and I laughed for nearly two hours watching Rachel being pulled from the hotel. And there she was, screaming that she was going to get you. I don't know how she figured that was going to happen, but she was. Then I think she saw the television crew." He asked his mom why they were there. "Not for her, though I think they did film her. That boy we hired, Jake, and his partner Forrest, they're making a name for themselves. I think you got the best of the best. But they were there for the unveiling of the plans for the new library addition. It's going to be nice. I think your boys had something to do with that too."

He hoped they were doing a good job. He would hate like hell to have to turn his son over to that monster. Brody hadn't realized how much he'd had riding on this. There was his practice, his homes, money. Of course, she'd signed a prenup, but he knew that she was slick and would do just about anything for some money. But today was for Jordan.

The phone was ringing as soon as they entered the hotel room. Jake was on the line, and he sounded like a man who was either really pissed off or holding back on something. When he finally burst out laughing, Brody couldn't help but smile.

"Your soon to be ex-wife is on the line. Not with us at the moment, but as soon as I tell you a couple of things." Jake laughed again. "My God, Brody, I think she's more of a bitch than my ex-wife was. Does she by chance have any decorating skill?"

He had heard about Jake's wife. "I was afraid to give her

the chance. The house decorating was off limits to her at all times. What does she want, do you know?"

"Smart man. She said that she wasn't going to tell me, so I hung up on her. The second time she called, an officer was on the line. He asked me, politely, to let her talk to you so they could have some peace and quiet. I guess she's putting up a great big hullaballoo. I love that word. I might have to use it more often." Brody hadn't heard that word in a while either, and laughed. "Yeah, my grandma would say that a great deal. Anyway, I'll be on the line with the two of you. And since she's calling you from the police station, there will be someone listening in on that end and recording it. So, keep your cool and don't tell her anything that you'd not normally tell her if she didn't ask you. For instance, you can tell her about the tests, but only if she asks."

When the line opened up, the police officer said what Jake had told him. Apparently, Rachel was listening as well, but her end was muted. They told him they were recording the conversation, and that Brody's attorney was on the line as well.

"This is bullshit." The phone was muted when Rachel spoke; the small humming sound was all the notice that they got to clue them in on that. Then when she came back on the line, she wasn't any happier about having to behave, Brody would bet. "Brody, honey, I want you to get your rectum down here and bail me out. Give me a key to the house and stop this nonsense with our son. You know as well as I do that you're not going to go through with this. You need me."

"No." She asked him what that meant. "No, I'm not going to go and bail you out. No, I'm not going to give you a key to my home, and I'm certainly not going to stop with the proceedings. I'm divorcing you, Rachel."

"And you think that just because you have all the money,

you can do as you please? I'm your wife, you fucking dick shit—" The line went dead again, and Brody laughed. He wondered if Jake was laughing too when Rachel came back on the line. "I'm supposed to stop cursing. But I want you to know, Brody, that I'm calling you every name in the book in my head. Where is my son? I want you to make sure that when you go to court, or whatever the he...heck you think you're doing, you know that you're not going to raise him. He's our son, and as his mother, I'm the one that should raise him. Everyone knows that the mother wins in this sort of thing. I'm thinking now about how much me having our son in my possession is going to cost you."

"He is your son. You have that right, Rachel. And you know as well as I do that he's not my biological child. In fact, I found the list that you wrote on who could be his father." Brody looked at Jordan as he continued. "But I could care less who he was fathered by. He's my son, and I love him with all my heart. And as for you raising him, that's not going to happen either. You're neither a good role model nor mother."

"You have never had a heart, and you're abysmal in bed. Why is it you think I found other men to screw me? Because you might have a nice dick, but you hadn't a clue how to use it." Brody started to say that it might have been her, but he wasn't lowering himself to her level. "Don't you have anything to say? I have plenty, but I have to be nice. You have no idea what you're stepping into here by treating me this way. And tossing my parents out on their butts with nothing at all to fall back on."

"Perhaps you should have read the prenup better, Rachel. It stated that so long as we were married, I would provide your parents with a home to live in, as well as a car. The money allowance that I helped them out with was because, believe it or not, I'm a nice person." She snorted. "Regardless.

I've had enough. And since you've been stepping out on me since the day we married, I'm going to take back control of my life."

"Have you any idea how many men have fucked me in that big house of yours? Hundreds. Some days I'd take on two or three at the same time. It was so much fun, having men right under your nose." Again, he could have said more, but he didn't. "And with you all alone sleeping down the hall in your lonely little bed. Did you cry yourself to sleep, Brody? You pussy."

The line went dead, and Brody closed his phone when he heard a dial tone. It took everything that he had just to sit here and not hunt her down and strangle her. Then Jordan came to him and put his small arms around his neck.

"Dad, she's not worth it." Brody told him he knew that. "She's a mean person. And you are my dad. Can I tell you something?"

"Yes, Jordan, anything."

Jordan walked to the little cabinet that held snacks. He'd never taken anything out, but he knew that Jordan had a small sweet tooth. When he took out a candy bar, Brody smiled at him as he ate it.

"I found my birth certificate in Mom's purse when she took me to register for school a long time ago. I read it on the back too." Brody asked him if he knew what it meant. "I didn't. But I asked Clare, the girl next door. Dad, she has boobs and stuff. Anyway, she told me that my mom had been sleeping with other men, and you weren't on the list. I had to ask Grandma what sleeping around meant. She told me. I don't know why Mom would do that, do you? I just want you to know that I love you very much, Dad. And we're going to be all right."

"I agree. Any reason you didn't come to me with the

question?" Jordan's face turned red. "Are you afraid to talk to me about sex?"

"Gosh no. I know you know about sex. Geeze, Dad." They both laughed. "I wanted to ask someone that would tell me how it is. And boy oh boy, does Clare tell me like it is. But she said that I should ask you about it. I put my birth certificate in my baby book the day that we left the house. I wanted you to find it. I don't know who those guys are, but Mom wrote their names on the back of it."

Brody thought of the things that his son was figuring out. Sex. Stepping out. He was going to have to talk to him about other things, he knew — and soon. But what he really wanted to do was let him know that he could come to him about anything. Even if it might embarrass them both.

"Thank you." Jordan threw the rest of the candy in the trash. Looking at his phone again when it rang, Brody realized that they had to get to the airport. It was Jake. "We're headed to the airport now, Jake. Do you think we can talk when I get there? I'm beat after that. And Jordan is as well."

"Yes, that's a wonderful idea, Brody. I'm so sorry about all this. I know just what you're going through." He thanked him. "All right. I'll see you, I guess, around seven tonight. Enjoy your flight, and remember, there will be a car at the airport for you when you arrive."

~*~

Emmi watched the planes land and take off. Damn it, she wanted to go home and curl up on the couch, take some pain pills, and forget the world. Why Aaron had to come home right now was driving her nuts. But then, everything drove her nuts lately.

Aaron had a good job, one that would take him all over the world one week then he'd be off for a while. And when he was off, if he could, he'd stay with her. Usually it wasn't any trouble. But she knew as soon as he saw her body — because she knew that she wasn't going to be able to hide her pain from him — he'd have a major shit fit, and then she'd have to explain things that she didn't know.

She saw that her brother's plane was on time and would be landing in twenty minutes. Emmi sat back down in the chair, extremely careful of how she sat, and then leaned back. Then she began to think and wait again. Closing her eyes, she tried not to think of anything, to make the pain go away. Drawing — or painting, it mattered little to her. But she enjoyed it so much that sometimes she could forget about the world and the way that it had been shitting on her lately. Emmi remembered to check the flight times again and the gate where he'd be coming in. When she opened her eyes, however, a small boy was standing nearby.

"Can you help me?"

She was leery of the kid. Not just him, but all kids. This was some sort of scam, she knew it. Looking around, she asked him where his parents were.

"My mom is in jail and my dad and I are coming here to live."

Too real to be a lie, Emmi thought. But that didn't mean she wholly trusted him yet.

"Okay. And why are you not with him? I mean, you don't look old enough to drive or anything yet. What gives?" He cocked his head and stared at her. "Kid, I don't know what your deal is, but I don't want to have to be dragged off to some sort of chamber and have someone kill me. Tell me what's going on. And no lies. Okay? I've had a shitty day — well, month — and really, I just want to go home."

"My dad said that the car was going to be here to get us, but I had to go to the bathroom. Dad said that he did too, so we went inside." He pointed to the men's room right behind

13

them. "Then when I was all done, I washed up my hands and came out to stand by the door. But he never came out. I think that my mom escaped and she's killed him."

"Kid, you have a great imagination." He told her his name. "All right, Jordan Downs. Let's go see what we can find out. To be honest, I got trapped in that bathroom crap too. It opens up on both ends. I came out on the wrong side and was lost for a bit. Come on, we'll get this figured out."

He took her hand into his and she froze up. Emmi didn't care to be touched, especially when she was hurting as badly as she was at the moment. People terrified her, especially men. She supposed it was because of her husband when he found her. But knowing why she didn't care for it didn't make her any less unhappy about being touched.

Emmi was married—or so she'd been led to believe. She didn't remember the wedding, the man, or for that matter, what he looked like. But she was getting these summons— bills—that were apparently made by her husband that she had to pay. Not to mention, someone had changed her name on not just her mail box, but also her monthly bills, like rent and her utilities. No matter how much Emmi searched for some clue, she—

"Are you all right, lady?" She told him she was fine and her name. "That's a pretty name. I'm betting it's short for something pretty too. Dad said he didn't want me to have a nickname. He thought them to be confusing to little kids. People think sometimes I'm a girl. I'm not."

"Yes, I can see that. There are all kinds of names that are gender neutral. You said that your dad had a car waiting on you? Do you know if it was a rental or a bigger car?" He told her. "I see. So, the person coming to get him might be at the gates with a sign for this limo. And if your dad is there, problem solved. If not, we'll try out plan B, where we have to

14

involve the airport security. And just between the two of us, I don't think we'll get too much help from them either."

She was hurting; trying to find the little boy's dad was pulling on stitches and bruises that she had all over her body. The airport wasn't that long, but there were a lot of people walking into them. Pay attention to your surroundings, she wanted to scream at people. But she—

"You sure do walk fast." Emmi slowed down. She had very long legs, and she'd forgotten for a few minutes that she was with a kid. "Thanks. Look over there. See those big signs?"

"I do."

She was nearly to them when she was thrown to the floor and someone had her arms too far up her back. Airport security was screaming at her to get away from the boy.

Emmi hadn't a clue how that was to happen, as she had an elephant of a guard on her aching back. It was all she could do not to pass out. Not to puke where she lay. Then man on her, because there was no doubt to her that it was a brute of a man, was telling her to not move, not to say a word.

She was sick with the pain, and Jordan was screaming at them to let her go, that she was helping him. Before she could beg anyone for help, any kind of help, she was let go and yanked up to her feet. Emmi had to lean over until she not only caught her breath, but the pain was gone—which by her estimations, would be never. No longer able to hold onto the bile in her empty belly, she turned her head and dry heaved for a few minutes. The shoes in her view were expensive and polished. There was only one person that she knew who had shoes that shiny.

"Hello, Aaron. Don't touch me yet." Laughter had her peeking up at her brother. "I was only trying to help the kid. Now I have to go home. You're on your own to get there. In fact, you should maybe go back to where you were for about ten years."

"I heard the kid. Christ, I think the entire place heard him telling them that you hadn't done anything wrong. However, I did not know that you were in so much pain that you should have told your big brother." She wanted to wipe at her nose and tears, but she hurt too much. "I'm going to find out what happened—you know that, don't you? In the meantime, do you need something for the pain, Emmi?"

"I'll be all right. Just give me a minute. Could you help Jordan find his dad? He said he was getting a car." Emmi couldn't move, but she had to sit down. Trying to lower herself to a better position was making her sicker. "Aaron, I'm not going to be able to move without help. Can you sit me on the ground? There is a better place for me to die, I think."

"No dying, Emmi. I mean it. And so you know.... Well, that's for later. Where can I touch you?" Aaron's voice was so strong that she wanted to lean into it, much like she had as a child when she'd be taken to task about something made up by her parents that she'd done. But Aaron's shoes didn't move when she felt someone at her waist. "Don't touch her until she tells us where we can."

"She's bleeding." She heard Aaron cursing and the man behind her breathing hard. "Emmi, is it? I'm going to help you down to the floor. But you have to tell me where I can touch you. I think your brother is pissed."

"He's always pissed." Sobbing now, the pain was getting the better of her. "Find a gun. Shoot me between the eyes and I'll feel much better." She heard Jordan tell them no. "I was kidding, Jordan. I just hurt too much right now to think of anything other than not being in pain. Just leave me here. I'll move when I'm able."

There was a pinch at her arm. Before she could turn, if

16

she could have, to see what had happened, the man behind her came into focus. He was rubbing a place where she was sure that he'd drugged her. Then, amazingly, she started to float away.

Emmi was never one to be able to just take a pain pill or shot and be able to be pain free. She was a redhead and all that came with it—freckles, pale and sensitive skin. If she was out on a beach for ten minutes, she'd be burnt to a crisp. Like she'd ever been to a beach, she thought with a smile. Then she heard Aaron tell whoever had shot her up that she was indeed a redhead, and she felt another pinch to her skin, then absolutely nothing.

There were glitches in the things that she saw when she woke. A giant cat—a tiger, she realized. Then there was a man, telling her she was all right. Over and over Emmi thought that she'd died only to wake a little to more pain. When she was finally able to focus on her surroundings, there was a man in the room with her doing a crossword puzzle. As she watched him, he cursed at the clues.

"What the hell is a steam engine scoop? You'd think a man my age would have heard it all. Stupid puzzle." Clearing her throat twice, she told him the answer. "Bucket, huh? Let me look. Yes, that's it. Thank you. I would have given up had I not been assigned to watch over you. Though I must tell you, it's not a bit of hardship on my part."

"You're babbling, and I hurt. Where am I?" The man stood and stretched. Her mouth went dry as the shirt he had on pulled up from his pants. Looking away, Emmi saw that she had an IV, as well as that her body was layered in gauze. She was in the hospital someplace. "Where is Aaron? I'd like to go home now."

"If you mean your brother—who is very scary by the way, even for me—he and a couple of other guys went to the cafeteria for something to eat. Do you need for me to get you something for pain?" Shaking her head, she closed her eyes. "Yes, well, you might want to talk to the doctor before you start moving around too much. Brody said you were a bitch to put back together. Who did this to you?"

His voice had gone hard, and she turned to look at him again. There was something about him, something that made her think she knew him, but her head hurt too much to be able to remember.

"You never said where I was. And who the hell is Brody?" He sat down, picking up the puzzle that he'd been working on. "Okay. Be a shit. I'm getting out of here."

When she sat up, costing her everything that she had in her, he growled low. It took her a moment to realize that he was growling at her. But for some reason, she wasn't afraid of him—more like pissed off. So Emmi did what she wished she'd done to her dad every time he'd drawn back to hit her. She doubled up her fist and socked him right in the nose.

# *Chapter 2*

Brody laughed every time he saw Quincey. Emmi Wright had blackened both his eyes and broken his nose. And because she was his mate, he couldn't heal until she forgave him, which didn't look as if it was going to happen anytime too soon. They were alike, the two of them, he'd come to surmise—stubborn, loud, and didn't care who was around when they voiced their anger. Brody was having a good time.

"I don't think this is funny. You do know that I could kill you in a way that would make you suffer endlessly?" Brody laughed again, just a short burst of it, and nodded. "Have you found out anything about the man that is going to be dead soon? Whoever injured her, he is going to pay for this. Firstly because she's my mate, and secondly, no one should hurt anyone like he did her, especially a woman. It looked to me as if he beat her with a cat-o-nine tails. Do you know the strength it would take to live through what she suffered?"

"No. I don't know anything more about her than you do. She was hurt, and helped my son regardless of the pain she was in. Also, Quincey, I don't want you upsetting her anymore. Did you know that I had to put in seven more stitches because of you pissing her off?" Quincey said that he was sorry. "I know she's your mate, but if you upset her anymore, she'll disappear. Her brother said that she's very good at hiding from those she doesn't want to see."

Brody wondered about the man who had hurt her. Why was he doing this to Emmi? And by the looks of other wounds on her body, he'd been doing it repeatedly for some time now. He'd not told Quincey about it, but he had a feeling that the man already knew it.

"I can find her, no matter what, because I have her scent and a taste of her skin. Had you allowed me to, I would have healed her completely. But I do understand about the police needing to see what had been done to her. Also, I do thank you for allowing Forrest to seal up the worst of the wounds, but she is still in pain and my beast is aching to heal her."

Brody had gotten a crash course in mates when he arrived. He'd known about shifters and mates, just not the totality of it all. Like, wounds given by a mate, and how they would heal or not. Brody had supposed, because of what he'd been told, that mates didn't or even couldn't hurt their other half. But now he knew that when they did, it would be a wound that would stay forever until forgiven for the misdeed. Such as, Quincey scaring Emmi to the point of her hitting out.

He laughed again on his way back to the meeting he'd been in when Quincey told him that Emmi was awake. Jordan was staying with Forrest for the afternoon, while Brody would get the lowdown on his divorce proceedings as well as care for his very first patient here. So far, he was happy with both.

"Is she all right?" He nodded and told them about Quincey. "Yes, well, who knew after all this time that he'd find himself a second mate? And a hellion to boot. I've only been around her when she's out, but from what Aaron told me, she's nothing short of a marvel on feet."

Brody had yet to meet the young man. He'd been at the airport when he and Jordan had been, but with his sister being in so much pain at the time, they'd not been introduced nor did they talk, other than for Aaron shouting at Brody for not helping her enough. Then here at the hospital, it had been nonstop busy with getting registered, taking care of Emmi, and setting up a place for him to have an office, as well as a room for Emmi. He supposed that easing into things wasn't in the books right now.

Brody looked over the paperwork that Jake handed him.

"All the locks have been changed, as you know. And the things from the house that your mom wanted are all on a couple of trucks. It'll be here in a couple of days." He thanked him. "No need for that. Forrest did the same for me when I was getting ready to get away from my wife. Anyway, since you're only moving from a couple of towns over, you can keep the same banks. And they're aware that she can't get into your accounts. I know you had that set up before, but now they know that they'll be responsible for it if she does. Not that she hasn't been in there trying. I guess it's her thing to make a ruckus wherever she goes. But she didn't get anything from them. And of course, if she had any credit cards, they won't work either."

"My mom, when she was packing up Rachel's bedroom, found stashes of money all over the place. Also jewelry and other items that were bagged up to be taken. She thinks that she was hoarding things to make a fresh start when she left me." Jake said that sounded about right. "And the article that you put in the paper — the one about her being responsible for her own debt. It's working out too?"

"Yes. Her boyfriend — I think his name is Ralph Comings — he's been going around town since you left trying to raise the bail for Rachel. He's not doing such a good job of it, it appears. Apparently, and this might not be a shocker for you, your soon to be ex-wife isn't well liked." Jake laughed. It wasn't the first time since he'd been sitting with this man that he had, and Brody relaxed. "It matters little anyway. She'll be getting out of the jail tomorrow morning. And she's going to be none too happy that her father is able to stay in the hotel that you have his wife in, and she can't. I have to tell you, that was brilliant."

"As much as I can't wait to be divorced from Rachel, my main concern is Jordan. Am I going to be his sole parent after this is all said and done?" Jake handed him another file. There were so many of them now, he'd need luggage to take them back to the hotel. "Who took these pictures of Jordan?"

"We got them off of surveillance cameras at the school. And you'll note the bottom of each picture that they're on the days that Rachel was to pick Jordan up from school. Also the times. And I checked, the times are accurate. Tuesdays and Thursdays were her days, correct? Your mom, you told me, picked him up the other three days." Brody nodded as he looked at his son waiting for his mother in the clear pictures. He looked so sad, Brody thought. "Most of the time your mom came to get him when the school called. It was usually about two hours later than he should have been picked up. Rachel was about an hour late coming to get him all the other times. In fact, we couldn't find a single time when she was on time to get him. The school takes notes about that sort of thing. Also, they have notes on who showed up when he was ill or there was a parent teacher conference. You never missed one. Rachel, however, never attended anything but plays. And usually she was dressed in something highly inappropriate for a class function."

"I remember those. Once she wore a red sequined dress to one of his Christmas plays, and yelled and whooped it up during the entire play. I believe she was drunk." Jake only nodded. "I'm sorry about all this. I truly am. I never should have married her. But I have to say, I honestly loved her — until we'd been married about a month and things started to become clear to me. Then it was about six years after I stopped sleeping with her that she told me she was going to have a baby."

"Don't worry about it, Brody. My wife killed her mother because she wouldn't hand over any cash to her, and said to the police that she was doing her father a favor. Her mother was just too out of date when she went out, and it didn't reflect well on her when she did that." Brody said nothing. He'd heard a little about Carol Winslow. But he was getting firsthand information now. "We'll get this taken care of, and then we can talk about the job here. The one, I might say, that you're doing very well for not having one."

"Jordan loves the school that you got him into. At first, I have to say, I was a little nervous about him being around wolves. But he comes home every day less tense and more happy. When my mom gets here, she's going to be very thrilled that we took precautions to keep him away from Rachel." Jake told him that he was afraid she'd try to take him for money. "I have no doubt about that now. She's a sick bitch."

They were going over some of the things Brody had yet to get done when his cell phone rang. It was his mom. She and Howie were nearly there but were stopping for some lunch, then heading the rest of the way home. He looked at the time and realized how late it was getting, and he'd had plans to go with Jordan to check out a house.

"Emmi wants me to release her. But to be honest with you, I'm afraid that whoever is hurting her will find her. Have you been able to find out anything?" He said that Cattie,

Cam's sister, was looking into it. "I heard that she and Cam were both good. And he's now in charge of the FBI unit in this area."

"Yes, that's why you've not met him yet. And if anyone can find out what Cattie can't, it'll be him. I have a feeling that it's a husband or boyfriend that is stalking her. And no matter what she does to hide from him, there he is." The next time he found her, Brody thought, she'd be dead. He told that to Jake. "Not if Quincey has anything to do about it. The guy is on pins and needles trying to figure out how to talk to her. It's killing him to see her in pain, and more so that she kicks him out of her room when he tries to come in."

Quincey was a very old and very powerful vampire. For a while, Brody heard, he and another vampire had been living with Cam's mom. But now that he'd found Emmi, Quincey had been staying someplace else. The only vampire that Quincey knew that was older than him, Jake told him, was his maker, Howard. They didn't have last names, the two of them, so took on those that suited them when they were required to have one. Quincey, he told him, was going to be called Quincey Wright, like his mate, Emmi.

Driving home, he talked to Jordan. He was very excited to have his grandma nearly there. Brody was happy that they had such a tight relationship, and wished every day that he'd had the same with his own grandparents. But they had died before he'd been born.

Pulling up in front of the big house that was Jake and Forrest's, he was envious of how nice the place was. His house at home hadn't been that large, but it had been big enough for him to have guests over to stay, as well as room to keep away from Rachel. Squashing that thought in favor of his son, who joined him on the porch, Brody thought that this was the highlight of his life — having a son that loved him as much as

Jordan did.

Of course the two of them were invited to dinner, and when his mom showed up with Howie, they were invited for dessert, as they were too tired for a whole dinner. Howie looked exhausted, but Mom looked like she could have talked all night. Brody asked Howie if he was all right.

"Yes, sir. Just fine. Ready for my own bed—and a meal that doesn't have a wrapper around it. Not all the food we ate was like that, but it sort of spoils the good stuff for you." Brody asked him if he'd feel like going to see the houses tomorrow. "I'd see them now, I'm so ready to put down some roots. Oh, by the way, your mother and I, we bought us new phones. Rachel has been calling the other phone numbers and leaving nasty messages. I'll give you the new numbers."

Jake overheard the conversation and asked if he could have the old phones. After Mom dug them out of her purse, she handed them over to him. They also made plans to go and see the two houses that had been purchased by Jake and Forrest in anticipation of Brody's family coming here to live. Loading up in the car, Mom talked a mile a minute to Jordan about their trip, and Howie—he wondered if he'd get used to that name—was telling him about how the furniture was coming in two days. They were about set, as far as he could see.

The first house Jordan didn't like. He didn't have a reason for it, but he didn't care for it. He said vibes, whatever that meant to a five-year-old. And Mom said that there wasn't a picture window to show off the tree in. Jake was still laughing as they loaded up again to see the next house.

Brody watched Jordan with Christy. She was so pretty and childlike, but he knew that she was in her thirties. She had the most adorable laugh that he'd ever heard. It just made his heart sing when she giggled. And Jordan was becoming a pro at making her laugh.

The next house came into view, and Mom and Jordan both said that this was it. Christy said that this house was a good one too.

"How do you know? You've not even stepped foot into it." Jordan got out of the car and ran up to the porch. It was a wraparound sucker that was almost deep enough to park a car on. And as soon as he put his hands on the railing leading up to the beautiful porch, Brody knew that it was going to be their home. He could feel it too, the vibes, as Jordan called them. "I have to admit, I can feel it too. Good sensations here."

His mom agreed even as they walked into the front entrance. It opened up into the large hallway that had a curved staircase that seemed to go on forever. Howie didn't stay with them — he wanted to check out the kitchen — but the rest of them went from room to room while Jake told them what he knew about the house.

"It did have ten bedrooms, believe it or not. But the previous owner wanted more space in the rooms, plus a couple of bathrooms down the hall. The master suite is bigger than a garage, and has a four-poster bed in it. They couldn't get anyone to move it. I guess it's extremely heavy." They were in the library now, and he could picture his books, which he had a great many of, on the shelves. The tall windows would let in enough light that he could sit there all day and never turn on a light. "At one end of the hall, there is the master, as I said, but the other end boasts one as well. Same layout, but slightly smaller. And they both have large walk-in closets."

Mom was going on about the closets, but all Brody could think about was that it was going to be a home for Jordan. A place, with the fenced in back yard, where he could go and play. A pool for the summer months, and a nice big deck that was surrounded by trees. This place had it all, and he was in love with it.

Jake came up behind him while he was staring out at the back yard. "You like this one, don't you?" Brody nodded. "It's not far from the hospital. The clinic that you can open, if you wish, isn't that far either. Both within walking distance. There is a library, too, that we're getting updated, and the pack ground butts up against this yard and ours. The gatehouse that we passed will be manned as soon as you take possession, and there are any number of pack and other shifters on this land, and all the others, all the time. Your neighbors to your left are Cattie and Tyson. They're trying to have a baby now too."

He turned to thank him in time to see him and Forrest, who had come along too, holding hands. It didn't bother him—in fact, Brody felt jealously, something that he'd never felt for another person before. Nor did it bother them at all when they kissed. They were mates, in love, and Brody was as envious of that as he was anything he'd ever thought of before.

"I don't mean to be rude, and please, if I'm sounding like it, it's because I'm curious. There are a lot of same gender couples around here. I take it that the town is very accepting of that." Forrest told him that he wasn't rude at all, and said that they were. "I'm glad. I've seen a lot of people come in through the ER with wounds from people taking exception to what sexual orientation they were. None of them were small ones, either. And the fact that it would be that one thing that bothered a perfectly normal person, enough to drive them to maim and kill, never set well with me."

"Our parents weren't at all accepting, neither mine nor Jake's. But since mine are dead and Jake's dad is in prison, there isn't anyone that gives us any trouble. A few weeks ago, we had trouble with our neighbor. We all thought it was

27

because we were gay. But it turned out he was wanting to kill us so that he could cash in on what he thought we were doing here—running a hotel. He's moving on. Quincey convinced him that he'd live a good deal longer if he did." Brody had no issues with anyone and what they did behind doors. "What do you say we figure out the paperwork before your mom has the furniture all in place even before the trucks get here?"

It didn't take them long to sign a rental agreement. It would be better if he didn't own anything right now, he'd been told. That way it wouldn't appear on any records where he was, and Rachel couldn't claim that he'd purchased it for her. That would be something that she'd do, too. After that, they all headed to the hotel to play around in the indoor pool and have some beers. It was a good night for that, and Brody was looking forward to having celebrations in their new home.

"Dad?" Jordan joined him in the living room of the suite they were in when everyone returned to their homes, and hugged him before having a seat. "Mom, she's not going to come here, is she?"

"I don't know, Jordan. But you do know that you're safe where you are during the day, correct?" Jordan nodded and laid his head on his chest. "You just have to do what they tell you to do when they tell you and you will be all right. Besides, you and I, we have a lot of things to look forward to, don't we?"

"Yes." Jordan yawned. "I don't want her to come here, but I know that she will. She was always telling that Ralph person that you owed her. I don't know what she meant, because you gave her lots of stuff."

"I gave her too much, I think now." Jordan said he might have. "Are you going to be like your grandma all the time and tell me like it is, instead of fibbing just a little?"

"Yes. Mr. Henderson said that I could call him Grandda if I wanted. He's a hoot, huh?" He thought that him and Ann both were—they were grandparents to Cam and Cattie. And for being in their nineties, they were in excellent shape too. "He even told me that he would keep me safe too. We're going to go for ice cream tomorrow, and he's going to show me the highlights of the town. He said that there weren't that many, but he'd be happy to show me."

"You remember what I told you about being out with him." He said that Grandda was frail and to not get too jumpy around him. "Yes, well, I didn't say jumpy, but that covers it too."

"Dad, what's an immortal?" He told him to the best of his knowledge. "He's one. Grandda and Grandma, my new ones, are both immortals. I'm glad that they'll be around forever. It'll be good to have someone to go fishing with, I think."

Jordan went off to bed then and left Brody thinking about what he'd just told him. Immortal? He knew that Quincey and Howard were, being vampires. But the elderly man and woman? Brody wasn't sure what to think about that. It wasn't as if he didn't believe him, he was just unsure where he'd gotten it from.

Turning off the light in his room, he moved his son over to get into the bed. The kid had a perfectly good bed and he was sleeping with him again. Smiling, he got in and was promptly hit in the face. Jordan wasn't one to understand sides on the bed, apparently.

His phone woke him up at nearly one in the morning. Answering it with his name, he was surprised to hear the panicky voice of Emmi. He told her to calm down and he'd help her.

"There's a woman here in the hospital. She knows that you're around here, and she's looking for you. Everybody is telling her that you're not here, but I think she's off her rocker." He asked if she knew her name, even as he was pulling on his pants. "I don't know, dumbass. She's screaming at the top of her lungs about you. We haven't gotten around to exchanging email addresses and phone numbers. Are you coming here or do I need to call someone else? Christ, she's getting closer."

"Go to the bathroom and lock the door. I know you can get around better, but please don't hurt yourself." He thought she said something nasty to him, but he chose then to ignore it—something about his ass and shoving something up it. "I'm on my way. And I'm calling the police."

He also called Jake to let him know. He sounded as if he'd been awake, and told him that Jenna had needed him when he asked if he had awakened him. Jake said that he'd send Forrest and things would work out. He hoped so. He only had one patient right now, and he didn't want anything to happen to her.

The place was a madhouse when he arrived. The police were there, and it looked like the entire department had shown up. As he made his way to the second floor where Emmi was, it turned out that she had disappeared. Before he could panic again, Quincey appeared before him.

"I have Emmi. She's safe." Brody nearly fell over, he was so relieved. "She's not happy, as you can well guess, but she is not going to be hurt. I will return her, if you wish, but for now, I'm trying to have a conversation with her that doesn't end up with me having a stake through my heart. It can no longer kill me, but I think she would give it a good try, don't you?" Quincey was smiling, and in turn, Brody did as well.

"Thank you so much. And I think you might be correct on the murdering part. She's a tad touchy, isn't she?" He nodded and disappeared again. The police were coming toward Brody when he realized that he'd not asked Quincey where he'd taken Emmi. "Did you find Rachel?"

"No, sir. We've searched the entire hospital and she's not here. We have patrols out searching the grounds for her now." Brody thanked him. "Sir, if I were you, I'd find someplace better and safer to live than a hotel. It's a nice place, but the security isn't as good as you need."

"I have a house, just waiting on our things to arrive." Brody looked around at the damage that had been done to the walls. "I'll be happy to pay for this. Who do I have to see to make sure that it's done?"

"I'd wait on that too, if I were you. We need to get someone in here to take videos of it, as well as pictures, and he's not able to come for a few days. Once we have it done, I'll talk to the head of the hospital and tell them what you said. I know you're divorcing her, so I'd keep track of all you spend on cleaning up her mess if I were you." Brody thanked the man again. "Dr. Downs, she sure has a hard-on in finding you, doesn't she? If you don't mind me saying, I think you're a lucky man to be getting distance between her and yourself."

"She doesn't like that I didn't care for her sleeping with other men in our bed, or that I took her money away. Rachel seems to think what is mine is all hers." The officer said that he'd met a great many women and men like that in his job. "I bet you have. And I thank you for helping me out with this. I'll talk to Jake when we're done here, and see what else we can do to keep the people working here safe."

"We appreciate that. We do. And if you find that you need to find yourself something else to do—doctoring, I mean—we're in need of a police physician. You'd go on calls with us, and help us out with cause and time of death. The last man we had retired a few months ago. We have a part time coroner, but he's getting ready to hang up his hat for a fishing pole too. I didn't realize how much we needed him until he

31

was gone." Brody wondered if the man was serious. It was his dream job to work with the police on cases. "You let me know and we'll get you set up. I've heard nothing but good things around here about you."

Cleaning up what he could of the things that had been destroyed in Emmi's room, he was able to bag up her things after one of the men took pictures of the things that had been messed with. There was not really that much except clothing and her shoes, but Rachel had done this to get back at him somehow. And now she was close enough that he'd have to worry all the time about his son. Nothing else mattered but Jordan right now.

The sun was coming up by the time he was pulling in the drive. Mom met him in the parking lot—she was headed next door with Jordan and Howie to have a fine breakfast— fattening was what she meant. Brody joined them, and didn't mention what he'd gone out for other than he had been needed at the hospital.

The cruisers that went by the restaurant were great. He tried to relax and eat, but it was difficult when he kept looking over his shoulder all the time. Finally, when his mom pointed it out to him, Brody shook it off. What could Rachel do in broad daylight?

Mom got a call from the movers just as he was paying the check. Thankfully, their things had arrived a day early, and he was almost too excited to drive.

Calling Jake, as he'd been told to do, by the time they got to the house there were thirty or so men there to help unload the trucks. Not only did they get the trucks unloaded in an amazingly quick time, but they were willing to help them place things in the rooms too. Jordan was having his bed put together when he found him in his room.

"Tomorrow we'll go and get you a computer, all right?

And a few other things that you need." Jordan was so happy that he wanted to take him out today. "How about we invite everyone over tonight for a lot of pizza and desserts? Howie said that he could hire us a cook in the morning, and we'd be having good meals all the time."

"You know, that's good. I'm a little bit tired of eating out all the time. They treat me like I'm a baby." Brody smiled when he thought of the way Jordan had pouted when they asked him if he wanted a lid on his cup. "Do you think that Howie was serious, Dad, when he said he'd get me some lids for here?"

"No, he wasn't. But you have to pretend with him for a little while. You know how much he loves to tease you." Jordan rolled his eyes, a habit that he was sure he'd picked up from Brody's mom. "All right. I'll be in my office trying to get it squared away. You come there if you need me."

"I'll be okay. Taylor here, he's going to show me how he fixed up his room at his home. You should see it, Dad. It's really neat." He nodded and said that they'd talk about it later.

Brody loved the house. And in less time than he thought it had taken them to pack, it looked like they'd lived there for years instead of just a little while. Mom was directing three men in where to hang the pictures, and he even had a throw over the back of the large sectional that fit perfectly in the room. He talked to Henry, who was helping out too, and asked him about dinner.

"Hell yeah, that'll be wonderful. And Christy, you know her, she and I have some things to talk to you about too." He could only imagine what the man had to say. "It's not bad. I promise you."

"I think I've had a pretty good day so far, so this might be the perfect time to get me up to date on the rest of the group." Henry told him to keep an open mind. Brody wasn't sure what that meant, but told him he would.

There were boxes everywhere in his office, but it wasn't daunting as it might have been to some people. It just meant to him that he could start fresh in here—put things where he wanted them and fill the shelves with things that were personal to their new life. And he was sure that he and the rest of his little family would make a great many memories too—memories that would sustain him until he was pushing up daisies.

The first thing he put on the shelf was a picture of him and Jordan. The second on was of Ms. Little. He missed the cantankerous old woman every day.

# *Chapter 3*

Rachel was as pissed as she'd ever been. Going by her home, she found that not only was the place empty, but no one could tell her where they'd gone. And the large For Sale sign out front with a glaring Sold on it made her want to destroy it.

She had a feeling that they might know where Brody was, but for some reason had decided not to tell her. Throw a couple of loud parties and people held it against her, just because she'd told them to fuck off when they told her to turn it down.

It wasn't as if she wanted to stay married to Brody. No, never that. She didn't like him anymore than he did her, she supposed. But she did want money, and she'd get it from him in any way that she could at this point. Rachel wanted a life, her own life, and in order to get going on that, she needed cash. And a great deal of it.

"Where the hell are you living, you piece of shit?" There were all kinds of little places that he could have been staying — bed and breakfasts out the ass; hotels that she'd been barred from when she'd let it slip that she wanted her husband dead.

35

KATHI S. BARTON

There was nothing for it—she had to find him in order to get what she needed. And as much as she needed the kid, she'd already decided that if she won custody of him—and she didn't think that was going to be a problem—she didn't want him around. Rachel had hated the town they'd lived in. It was small, with no malls worth her time. Only a few restaurants, and they were just chain places. And this town, just down the road from the other one, where she'd figured out he'd gone, wasn't any different—small and drab. But she knew that it'd be just the place for Brody. He loved small towns.

Her cell phone had been cancelled. And when she'd gone by her mom's place to get hers, she saw that it was empty too. Christ, they must have had trucks on standby to pack up the houses. There wasn't even a little flag thing that her mom so loved to put in the flowers. Christ, it was more dreary looking than before, she told herself.

It took her all of a day to find her mom. And to find out that she was living it up in a hotel wasn't something that she wanted to hear about.

"You can let me stay here for a few days, right? I mean, I literally have nowhere else to go." Her mom stood in front of the door, barring her from entering. "Mom, I'm not in the best of moods here. Get out of the way and let me in. I need a shower and money. Please tell me that Brody left you some cash."

"He didn't. But if we want to stay here for the time we have left, then we're not to let you come in at all. I sort of like that idea. I heard that you had a good time with some spray paint at Brody's home before the police caught you."

All she'd been able to paint on the house was an "S" for son of a bitch, and they'd made her clean that off too. She growled at her mother.

"Won't work, I'm afraid, Rachel. Because of you, I'm not

36

able to see my grandson, live in a very beautiful home, and have a car to drive around when I want. I never realized how much Brody was doing for us until you had a child that didn't belong to him. Oh, and let's not forget the affairs. Christ, Rachel, do you have any idea how much that man did for you? You should be horsewhipped for what you did."

"Look, I'm tired of debating how loving and wonderful my dick faced husband is. Just let me in, Mom. I'm not kidding you." Her mom said no, and just as Rachel was ready to barge in anyway, the elevator dinged and four officers got out. "You called the police on me? Mother fuck, Mom. Why the hell would you do something like that? I'm your daughter. You can't even let me in to get some money and a shower?"

"No. I told you, we're only here because we agreed to not allow you entrance. Rachel, I'm sorry to say this, but I'm glad that man left you. You aren't a nice person at all, are you?"

Rachel was escorted out of the hotel and told not to come back. Nearly spitting on one of the officers, after being warned that would get her prison time, she stomped away.

And now here she was staying in a fucking house that had nothing but a bed and a fridge. Ralph was certainly keeping a low profile in his choice of home, she thought. Looking at the road that as far as she was concerned was too close to the house, she frowned when Ralph asked her what her plan was now.

"Find him. And Jordan. He has to give me something. Even my clothing would be nice about now." Ralph had given her one of his shirts after she'd gotten a shower finally. "I had about a hundred grand stashed away in that place. And now there isn't even a planter on the front porch. I tell you, Ralph, the man is going to have to get his act together before things start to go badly for him."

Rachel wasn't entirely sure what she could do to Brody.

37

Not only did he have all the money, but he also could afford an expensive attorney, and had the ability to pack up two houses — in less time than she could have thought possible — and disappear from the fucking earth for a day and a half before she found him.

"I did find out that he was working at another hospital, didn't I?" She nodded. Ralph had, but it hadn't done her a bit of good. Not with him not there when she wanted him to be. "Next time you go and look for him, Rach, I'd suggest you go during the day. We both know that doctors never do anything full time, and they certainly never go out in the night anymore."

She'd not thought of that when she'd gone looking for him. Ralph had told her what he knew, and she took his car and went after Brody. Now she was not only barred from the hotel where her parents were, but the hospital had told her that they'd have her arrested on the spot if she returned, even if she was injured. Not nice, but she had made a horrible mess before leaving.

Sitting on the edge of the bed, she wondered what she was going to do now. No money, no clothing — not even a decent meal to be had. What really pissed her off about all of it was that she had a lovely home that her and Ralph had pooled their money to get, and the bank had seized it. She was still trying to figure that part out. It hadn't been Brody's, damn it.

"When do you have to go looking for a job?" He said in the morning. "I'd look too, if I had anything to put on. But they wouldn't hire me anyway, I don't think. I've made a nuisance of myself, I was told."

"We'll be all right. As soon as they figure out that the house doesn't belong to Brody, we'll have a nicer place to live. And since you had some of the things from the house put in it, we'll at least have something else to sit on than a bed." Rachel asked him what the banker had said about why they couldn't live there. "I don't know. Something about you taking money from Brody to buy it. But you told me it was your allowance, right? We used what he gave you monthly to get it."

"Yes." Another lie, she thought. Christ, she'd never had a job. Brody didn't allow her to use the credit cards he had. He'd buy her a prepaid card, and that was all she was allowed to spend. Like she was fourteen and didn't know the meaning of money.

But the house and getting it, Rachel realized, was going to be a problem. Not only had she taken things out of the house that belonged to Brody, but she'd used money that she'd stashed away every month by buying things then taking them back for cash. Yes, she supposed they had used his money. And that was going to be what his sharp assed attorney was going to tell her too.

"I can't even use the family attorney for this shit. He said that he didn't work for me, but for Brody. Mother fuckers, does the world work for him?" She didn't want to cry; there wasn't any way that she could repair what little makeup she'd been able to steal from the department store. As it was, the shit was cheap and didn't match her skin tone.

Lying down on the bed next to Ralph, she thought of Brody. Christ, he had a cock that was as big as her arm. And he did know how to use it, despite what she'd told him. He could make her come more times than all the men that she'd fucked put together. And when he'd cut her off, Rachel had been tempted to find her way into his bed again, just for some fun. But the fucker had locked her out of the room he'd been using since before Jordan had been born.

"I don't know if I'll be able to get Jordan after all this. If we don't, then we're screwed. He won't have to pay me a dime,

39

and knowing him like I do, he won't either." Ralph suggested again that they just take Jordan. "That is going to be another plan, I think. Jordan doesn't much care for me anyway, and if I take him and get caught, we'll both end up in prison. I need some money, but not enough to have to be in prison for the rest of my life."

"Too bad we can't hire someone to get him for us. I mean, just getting a million for us would be something to live on for a little while." She nodded, her mind thinking of who she might know who'd do it. "Do you have any idea who the baby daddy is? Maybe he'd do it, knowing that he's living with Brody and not you."

"There are four men that I think could have been his daddy. But I wouldn't even know where to find them now. I mean, they were, for the most part, one-night stands. It was fun, fucking people in that big bed, but I couldn't tell you where they were from, or even a phone number to call them."

Rachel hated to admit it, but she was fucked. And the fact that she hadn't planned better and gotten more money was all her fault. She'd seen that Brody Downs was a doctor, and dollar signs had gone off right before her eyes. Him having a medical degree should have tipped her off that he was smarter than she was thinking, but all she saw when she looked at him was handsome sap. And the ass hadn't aged one bit, so far as she could see, in the ten years they'd been married.

Looking down at her own body, she wondered what the hell had happened to her. She wasn't fat—plump was a word that she called herself. In reality, she'd gotten very plump over the years, and having the kid hadn't helped her figure either. But she'd been happy with the arrangement that they'd had—until Brody got a burr up his ass about her having affairs. What did he expect her to do, be celibate like he was? No fucking way.

40

Sex was fun. It was a way to escape from the world for a while. Coming hard, letting her body tense up then relax, had given her endorphins that she'd never had as a teenager. Rachel had been having sex since she'd been around twelve, when the boy next door, older than her, had introduced her to it.

Closing her eyes, Rachel tried to rest, to clear her mind. But all she could think about was how she'd messed up. Taking Brody for at least a portion of what he had wasn't working out in her favor. The man was worth billions, she thought, and she wasn't going to get anything of it. Even if Brody were to suddenly end up dead, she'd been told by his fucking lawyer, nothing came to her. Everything went to his mom.

Williemae — or Mrs. Downs, as she'd been ordered to call in her the last years of her marriage to Brody — hadn't liked her from the very start. Not only had she been mean to her about helping out with the wedding, but she had refused to throw her a shower when Jordan was born. The old biddy acted like this was all her fault, when Rachel was sure that some of it had to be lain at the feet of her precious son, Brody.

He'd been a jackass to her about catching her and Ralph in the bed together. Then when she'd decided to gather her shit, he'd locked it all away from her. Rachel wondered if even then he'd known what she was up to. Then there was him not allowing her to spend any time with her parents. Smiling, she wondered if he realized that he'd done her a favor. Rachel didn't like her parents any more than he had, honestly.

After a while, she tried to sleep. It was proving as difficult lately as it had been getting any money. Why, she wondered, wasn't she being thought of as the victim? Whenever her friends had gotten divorced, they'd had parties for the woman — given her advice on attorneys, for Christ's sake. All she got from the so-called friends when she went to them was doors slammed in her face.

Rachel was going to come out on top of this thing. She didn't have the slightest clue how that was going to happen, but by God, she wasn't going down without a fight. Brody would figure out that she wasn't nearly as dumb as he apparently thought she was. Rachel was smart and savvy.

~*~

Brody thought that the house was nearly finished. The pizzas and other things that Howie had ordered for dinner would be here in twenty minutes. Walking to the front door, he answered it himself, telling Howie that he had it. The man standing there was unfamiliar to him, and he felt his body tense up for whatever he had to harm him with.

"I'm Emmi's brother, Aaron Wright." Brody nodded but didn't move. "Am I too late for dinner?"

"No. No, I'm sorry. I have about a million things on my mind right now." Brody moved so that Aaron could join him in the hallway. "I might have met you at the airport, but I can't remember anything about you."

"That's fine. Emmi needed your attention more than I did. I'm only here for a few more days, then I have to leave again." He looked surprised, like he hadn't meant to tell him that. Jordan took that moment to come down the stairs to greet him. Brody introduced him to his son. "Hello, Jordan. I've heard a great deal about you. Emmi is my sister. She told me that you and her are going to be friends, she thought. I'd like that as well."

"We just moved in, and I have the neatest room. You want to see it?" Jordan was off with the man before Brody could object. For some reason, he didn't think that Aaron would harm Jordan, but he didn't know him at all.

While he was standing there debating whether or not

42

to go get Jordan, Henry and Patrick entered the house with Christy. She gushed over the house and everything, but she was strangely hesitant to leave the front hall. It wasn't until the rest of them showed up that she went to the living room. Then the food arrived.

He'd ordered twenty-five extra-large pizzas with a variety of toppings, but he did order six of them with all the stuff they could shove on one. The pizza place would become a favorite of his if the pizzas tasted as good as they looked. Digging in with the rest of them, he was glad that the table he had was big enough for all of them. Even little Jenna was enjoying her meal of peas and carrots. Jordan's new grandparents, Willy and Ann, even showed up, and it was a great way, he thought, to get to know everyone.

Conversation was light. Jordan joined in a lot, having an opinion about nearly everything. Wine was served to the adults, and he noticed that the shifters—he knew who they were—didn't partake of any.

"We don't get anything from alcohol. Drugs rarely affect us either." Jake looked over at his partner, and laughed before continuing. "I had no idea that a redhead would need more drugs. When I heard about it, I had to go and look it up. I guess there are a lot of things that don't work well on redheads."

Emmi showed up just as the conversation turned to talking about redheads, and she joined in like nothing was wrong. Quincey never left her side, and Brody could tell that it was annoying her. It was funny, really, to watch Emmi come to terms with the big man. Brody thought them to be a perfect couple.

"Did you know that you have a ghost with you?" No one stopped their talking, and he looked at Christy and asked her what she meant. "I don't know who it is. And I'm not allowed to ask them, but they've been hanging around you for some time. And there is one that was living here before you moved in."

"I don't know if you're serious or not." She said that she was very serious. "Why can you see them? I'm not saying that I believe you or not, but why is it that you can see them and I can't?"

"You've not become a family member yet. You and your mate, you have to find each other." He told her that he didn't want to find anyone else for his life. "I'm afraid that it's too late for that, Brody. He's here now."

He didn't want to think about finding another person to live with. Brody certainly didn't want someone in his life that was going to demand things —

"Did you say *he* is here?" Christy nodded, smiling at him. Brody leaned in closer to her. "Honey, I'm not gay. I have a son. I just left my wife, who was definitely female."

"So did Jake." Brody looked at the man across from him, talking quietly with Brody's mom. "You'll figure it out. In the meantime, the ghost that lives here with you, he'd like to ask you something. He said that its very important."

"All right. I don't know what I can help him with. As you know, I just moved in here today. And until the divorce is final and things are settled, I'm just renting this place from Jake and Forrest. After that, I can deal with the ghost because the house will be mine." Brody found himself glancing around the table. The only other male, besides him, that wasn't attached was Aaron, and he didn't strike him as a gay man. "What can I do for him? I don't want to be caught up in family drama right now. As I said, I don't own this house as yet."

"Oh, no. You couldn't do that anyway. There are rules that they learn when they pass over. I'm not sure how it works really, but they have them in their mind when they die." He nodded, not sure what he was to believe or not. "He

44

wants to know if you have been to the sublevels. I think it's the basement."

"No. I mean, I went down there, just to have a look around, but I didn't see anything. Please tell me that there's not a body down there and I'm not going to have to move again." Her laughter drew the attention of the rest of the table. After she explained to everyone what was going on, Brody went with her when she said that the ghost wanted to show her something. "Christy, if I find a body down here, I'm going to be sorely pissed off." She laughed with him.

They walked to where Christy told them. He hadn't been aware that almost everyone but him could see the dead man, and when he wondered on that, his eyes went to Aaron again. It was ludicrous, he thought, that this man or any man would be his mate.

"The ghost remembered his name. He said that he's Samuel Brown. And this, at one time, was his family home. He lived here until his family carted him off to a nursing home, where he died alone while they lived here in his home." Brody told the ghost that he was sorry. "He said that he is as well. They were looking for his stash."

Brody looked at the men and women in the basement with him when Christy started to explain. The ghost didn't want him to do anything for him other than to pull his stash from the wall.

"He said that at one time he was worth millions, but his family drained him day after day until they got tired of waiting on him to die. He said that before he left here, as they were making arrangements to move him out to die, he put everything that was his and his wife's, special things that they'd purchased for each other, in a leather bag and hid it here."

They found it without any trouble. Brody asked what he

was to do with it since Jake and Forrest owned the house. He was told that as far as they were concerned, it was his home. Christy looked to be listening to the ghost, and when she nodded, she smiled at him. "He would like for you to give it to your son. He said that he'd like to know that the pretties, as his wife called them, would be given to someone again. Someone that loved as much as he did his own wife."

Brody dumped the bag on the floor, and they all marveled at what was there. A diamond necklace; rings that were expensive as well as beautiful—their wedding rings, he'd bet—as well as other things that he'd stashed away so his greedy children, he called them, couldn't sell them off without regard to what their worth was to him and his wife.

Jake said that he'd look into it. If it was named in the will or the estate, then he'd have to find an owner, a relative. Mr. Brown told them that no one was left, but for Jake to go ahead. Drugs and alcohol had ended his family, he said, much too late for him.

He felt terrible for the gentleman, and told him that he'd do as he asked so long as there were no attachments to the things he'd told him about. When Christy looked at him again, she too had a sad smile and told him that the man had moved on.

"And the other ghost? What can I do for him? And to be honest with you, I'm a little leery of this, but I will help as much as I possibly can." Christy thanked him and told him the other ghost was his father. "My dad?"

He found himself on the floor. Brody wasn't sure how he'd gotten there, but he felt better there instead of standing. The others had left them, he noticed, except for Aaron. Brody wasn't sure if having him there was such a good idea, then Christy spoke again.

"He wants you to know that he loves you very much. Even

now." Brody nodded, tears filling his eyes. "He said that you might not have known it, but he was there on your wedding day and the day that you had your first delivery. He was also there when Jordan was born. Another wonderful thing that he thought he would miss. Mr. Downs said that he was proud of you, and spoke of you to anyone that would listen."

"He died before I was out of med school. And I was sad when he couldn't be at my wedding. Does he know that I'm getting a divorce?" Christy said that was why he was here. "Why for that?"

"There is information that you need to have. Mr. Downs said that he'd tell you in a moment. He said that I could call him Cain, if that was all right with you."

Brody nodded and took the hand that was offered. Aaron was lending him support, he told himself, but then he saw his father.

"I can see him." Christy welcomed him to the family. "I don't understand. Because my dad is here, I'm now a part of what you guys have?"

"No, because you found him."

Christy left them there, he and Aaron. He wanted to pull away, but he didn't. Looking at his father, he asked Aaron if he could see him as well.

"I can. And you look a great deal like him. Very handsome man." Both he and Dad thanked him. "Should I leave? Leave the two of you alone to talk?"

"No." Brody realized how he sounded. "No, don't leave me. I'm not sure what's going on right now. But please stay."

His dad sat with them. Not really on the floor, but he was trying, he told them. Dad smiled at them both before he spoke, and it was then that Brody realized that this was real. He was actually speaking to his father.

"How is your mother? I have to tell you, Brody, she was

47

the light of my life. Both of you were. I miss her, but I see her with you. Runs a tight ship still, doesn't she?" Brody laughed, and told him that she did. "You know that Jordan isn't yours, don't you?"

"Yes. We had tests done. I've known since he was born." Dad nodded and looked around the basement. "Please tell me that you don't have something that you wish for me to do and will then leave me. I have missed you so much, Dad."

"No, not today anyway. I just asked that young woman to help me, and I never dreamed that she'd make it so I could speak to you. It's wonderful." Brody wiped at the tears that were streaming down his cheeks. "I'll come to see you from time to time, son. This, you seeing and talking to me, it's draining. But I wanted to tell you about that person you married. My goodness boy, she sure had us fooled, didn't she? Anyway. About this thing that I know. When I was doctoring, before I retired, I had this acquaintance that told me that in order to make himself some extra money, he'd do some very nasty work on the side. He was someone that performed abortions on women who just didn't want to have a child. Sorry state of affairs, don't you think, when a person doesn't want their own child? But he kept records, and he made the women give him a picture of themselves. That way, he'd have a record in the event they were abusing his help, and he'd have a record of the person and their face so that someone else couldn't use their names. It was sordid, and I don't remember all the details as to why he did it. I sort of broke off talking to him too much. But he's still around."

"He has a picture of Brody's wife?" Brody looked at Aaron when he asked. "I'm sorry. This is private and I should keep my mouth shut."

"No. Don't do that. I don't know what's going on between us, and we'll talk, but for now, I'd like you to help me process this." Aaron nodded and Brody turned to his dad again. "This doctor — are you saying what Aaron did? That he has pictures of Rachel?"

"Oh yes. Several of them. While I'm terrible with timelines here on this side, I saw them when I was walking around his office not too long ago. I think there were dates when the two of you were married. But I don't know that for sure. You'll have to look." Brody got the address from his dad and asked him what else he wanted to do now that he could see him. "Just talk to you. That's all I ever wanted. And your mom too, if I'm able. Christy can help me out with that if you don't want to, but — "

"Dad, I would love to see you and Mom talking. But I do have to warn you. She and Howie — Howard, the butler. Remember him? — they've sort of hooked up." Dad laughed, and it brought to Brody a flood of memories of his dad laughing at different things. "You're not upset?"

"I am not. I'm glad that she moved on with her life. Howie? Never thought he'd allow himself to be called that, but then, a lot has changed since I passed on." He told his dad that it had been Jordan's idea. "I have to say, son, I love that boy. He's a good one too. But you might want to talk to him about that girl who lived next door to you. She was a little too blunt for that little fella."

Dad left then, saying that he'd stayed well past the time that he should have. When he faded away, he and Aaron sat there for several minutes, neither of them speaking. And when they went upstairs to the main floor, Brody didn't let go of his hand. Aaron held tightly to his as well.

# *Chapter 4*

Emmi wasn't sure what to do with this man. He was huge and she was in his home, but she didn't feel threatened at all by him. She did feel pissed off at him. The man was forever right up her ass. When he laughed, she looked at him, glaring.

"You have the thoughts of a murderous woman, when I know you have a heart of gold." She asked him what he was talking about. Could he read her mind? "Nay, I cannot, love. You are my mate. I can see your face, however. It is very telling. I'd not play poker with anyone, I believe the saying goes, if I were you. You would give away all our money."

"I don't have any money. Is that what this is about. You want my money?" Quincey told her that he didn't need it, nor did she. "I'm not sure if I want to believe you or not."

"I can understand that." He stood, his body mouthwateringly beautiful. "I can smell you, sweet flower. You smell of lust and need. I would love to give you relief from both."

"I'm married." He stopped moving, and she was disappointed. "I mean, I think I am. That's what the bank says about it."

51

"I don't understand." She said that she didn't either, but if he sat down and behaved, she'd tell him. "You say that a great deal, for me to behave. I'm not sure you mean it, to be honest. I would love nothing more than to take you to our bed and make love to you all night."

"Anyway." He laughed again, and her body heated with the sound of it. "I was at this party and something happened to me. I don't know what. Perhaps someone slipped something into my drink. I wasn't drunk—I don't drink—but that's what the police told me when I was picked up wandering the streets. I was also half naked."

"He did not rape you." She shook her head, and didn't even want to know how he came to that conclusion. "You smell beautiful, my Emmeline. And you are still a virgin. This night, why did they think you drunk? I'm sure that you are correct, you were given something."

"I was out, as I said. It was a celebration. All I was drinking was soda water. Not that I liked it, but it looked like an alcoholic drink, and I didn't have to explain myself to anyone who asked. But after I finished with the second glass, I began to feel woozy and odd." He sat down, pulling her into his lap, and with the comfort that she got from it, him simply holding her, she was able to tell him what she remembered. "I never told anyone else about this. It's not like I had a great deal to tell, really. I still don't remember a thing. But I have these wedding pictures. From Vegas. I've never flown before, either. My bills were changed. My last name was changed to Smith, of all names."

"How long before you woke up from the bar that night?" She told him it had been four days. "Four days of you having no memory of those days? Did anyone see if you had had your head injured? I'm thinking that they didn't believe you."

"No one did. And.... I paint, you see. And I was doing

52

really well with them up until this person, whoever he is, started taking money from my accounts. Getting charge cards in my name and charging up great amounts of money. I even got bills from Vegas, for the wedding and honeymoon suite. Even an apartment in New York. I don't even like New York." Quincey asked her if she was paying the debt. "Yes. I didn't want Aaron to know what was going on. This person, he beats the hell out of me too. I never see him. It's like I wake up in a fog and I'm banged up badly. But this last time...."

"I can look at your memories, Emmeline. I can see if you have any hidden memories of this person that would help me find him." Emmi looked at Quincey. He said that so calmly, like that would be all he did was to find him. But she had a feeling it was so that he could kill the man. "Yes, I will kill him. Not just for harming what is mine, but also for putting this stress on you."

"I don't know what to do. This last time, whoever did this to me, when I was in the hospital, the note told me that I wasn't to hide my money from him again." He asked her if she had the note still. Emmi went to her purse, the only thing that she had with her, and took it out and handed it to him. "I don't know what I can do with it. Or even you, for that matter. But I put it in that plastic Baggie as soon as I read it."

"You're very smart. Come here, my love. Let me see what else I can get from you. And I now have his scent. I can find him with that. But a memory of yours that perhaps might show his face would help me too." She sat next to him on the bed and he put his hands into her hair. "You are so very tense, Emmeline."

Quincey massaged her scalp, and untangled her hair from the tie she had it in. It was curly, she knew, and thought that he'd get his fingers all tangled up in it. But all he did was talk to her softly, his hands doing such amazing thing to her head

53

that she finally gave up and leaned into his chest.

"Close your eyes, Emmeline. Close them, and allow me to search your memories." She didn't know what he might see, but really, Emmi realized, she didn't care. "If you would allow me to nip at your flesh, I could find you if you should be lost to me. And we could communicate through a special link that would be all ours."

She didn't care what he did to her—her body was soft and mellow. She felt her pussy heat and swell when he brushed his fingers over her breast. Quincey was seducing her. Making her want him as much as he did her. Moving slightly on his lap, she felt his cock beneath her and moaned. When he slid his fingers to her heat and slid them into her, because all she had on was his shirt, Emmi felt the scrape of his teeth over her throat just before he bit her.

The climax was mind blowing. Every part of her body felt it. And when he cupped her breast in his hand, she wanted more, needed something that she knew only he could give her. When he turned her on his lap so that she was facing him, he held her there, not moving at all until she looked at him.

"I have bitten you so you're mine. But if I take you now, make love to you as we both want, we will be one. I will belong to you as much as you do me." She nodded. "No, Emmeline. If this happens, if you wish this, you must say the words. Say the words that will bind you to me. And I will do the same."

The words came to her. The declaration that she would say that would make her his forever. Not a lifetime—they would live forever. And when he kissed her again, it was with savagery, need, and something that she couldn't understand.

"It is love."

She nodded, and watched him as his body became bare to her. Emmi touched her fingers to his nipple, the hardness of it making her want more. Leaning to him, his cock thick between her nether lips, she bit down on his nipple hard enough to taste his blood. The shifting of her teeth felt odd at that moment, but she looked at Quincey and knew. She was in love with him.

"I, Emmeline Downs, will love you and only you, Quincey of my heart. I will feed you with my blood and my body. I will never hold back from you when you are in need." Emmi traced the long scar that went from his shoulder to his navel with her tongue. His moans fueled her own need until she was in pain from it. "I will love your children should we have any, from our bodies or not. You will be safe with me. I will tell no one where you live, where you reside except when necessary. Quincey, my one and only love, you have my heart, and I will hold you there for all time."

Lifting her up, he brought her down on his cock. There was no pain like she'd thought there would be. Nothing hurt when he filled her with himself. But when Emmi looked into his eyes, she knew that he'd made it possible for her not to be in pain. That her first time with him would be one of memories, not of pain.

They made love slowly. It felt like their bodies were getting to know each other. His hands touched her everywhere; the backs of her knees as he made his way up her body when he laid her out on the bed; her eyes; even her toes were suckled upon enough that she came with the sensations.

His cock filled her again and again. There was no rush for it. They were one now, had plenty of time to see what secrets they held for each other. She was bitten too. Every time he did, she'd come just a little harder, her body humming to what he was doing to her. And when he said it was time, she offered him her neck like she'd done it a million times. The bite, this time, would have her surrendering her life to her only love.

When she woke, she was alone in the large bed. It had to

have been special made for him. Quincey was at least seven feet tall, and his feet didn't hang off the end. Pulling the covers up over her nudity, she smiled when she saw him sitting in the dark, looking at her.

"I thought that I'd worn you out." Emmi told him that he had. "Good. And after you have rested sufficiently, I will wear you out again."

Emmi watched him, wanting him to come back to bed with her. He had something to tell her, but he was stalling. Not sure if she wanted to know or not what he was thinking, she asked him where she might find something to wear.

"There is a closet full of anything you wish to wear." Her heart hurt and she looked at him. "You have a look on your face that I cannot read."

"I don't want to wear the castoffs of your other women." He moved to her faster than she could see. When he had her pinned to the bed, she was afraid for a few seconds. "I'm sorry. Whatever I did, I'm sorry."

"You have no reason to be sorry, or afraid. I would never harm you. The clothing that I have brought here for you is yours. No one, I swear to you, no other person has been in my bed or left castoffs." She looked away and he brought her face back to his. "I have gotten them for you and only for you. If you do not care for them, then I will see if you have the same abilities as I do. I can dress myself in anything I wish. However, I must say, having you naked like this would be something that I'd like all the time."

Tears filled her eyes, and she felt horrible for saying something like that to him. She had only just sort of married him, and now she was insulting him. But when he took her hand to his heart, she thought of something to put on and was happy to feel the T-shirt and jeans cover her body.

"Alas, I guess you have the ability." He sat up, bringing

her with him. "Before I speak of this man, I must give you something. It is a token of my love for you. A wedding band, so that any humans who see you will know that you are mine."

The ring, if anyone could call such a piece as this only a ring, was beautiful. There was a large diamond on the top, and the wide band was made of platinum. She knew this because she'd studied jewelry for her work. When he kissed her again, gently this time, he told her what he'd been able to find out with the note the man had stupidly left her.

"I know his face too, but that's not important. He is a dead man, no matter how he looks. And you, my love, aren't the only one he's done this to. Mr. Fred Simmons, his real name, has even been to court." She asked him why he wasn't in jail. "I will find this out before I find him. And if I don't, then I will know after I touch him."

"He's done this to other women." He nodded. "No, please don't kill him. Not yet anyway. These other women, they were treated like I have been. Not knowing anything or why this happened to them. I want him to pay for this. Not just for me, but for all of them. They'll need closure as well. Don't you think?"

"You are correct."

She noticed that he would use contractions sometimes and sometimes not. She thought it had to do with his age. But he told her, when she asked, that it was because he was working to fit in with her life. Emmi had never been so happy about anything as she was now. She wasn't expected to fit into his life—he wanted to fit into hers.

"And I have seen your paintings. You are very talented. We will need to set you up with a place here to work, and bring some of your other works here. I wish to gaze upon them when you aren't close to me."

"Now you're just being sappy." She ran when he chased

her around the room. Giggling hard when he caught her, Emmi looked up at him when he took her to the floor. "You are the best thing that has ever happened to me, Quincey."

"And you to me, my love. You are the best that has happened to me as well."

She wondered about his first mate, the one she'd been told about, but now wasn't the time to ask. Not in their bedroom. Getting up, she went to find something to eat. Suddenly Emmi was starving.

~*~

Aaron hadn't any idea what to do—he wasn't gay either. But the thought of Brody touching him was making his cock hurt with need. Trying to reason with himself about what was going on, he looked up when Jake sat across from him.

"I have a feeling that you have about ten zillion questions right now. And just to let you know, Brody is having the same conversation with Forrest that I think you and I will have." Aaron nodded, then shook his head. "It's all right, Aaron. You're going to be fine."

"But I'm not gay." Aaron lowered his voice this time when Jake cocked a brow at him. "I've never slept with anyone but a woman. I wouldn't even know where to begin in making love to Brody."

"So you have thought of it." Embarrassed that he'd let it slip, Aaron nodded at Jake. "It's really not that much different than having sex with a woman. It's enjoyable. And if you do it right, very satisfying. We have breasts and sexual parts. And if you'd like to know, Brody is thinking the same thing. He's nervous as hell too."

Aaron got up to just move around. His body was tense with the thoughts that had been going through his head since he'd taken Brody's hand into his. There *were* about a zillion questions. But to put them into any kind of order, or to simply put them together coherently, was impossible at the moment.

"I have this job that takes me all over the world a great deal. I collect things — seeds, seedlings, and other species — that are having issues. Such as, they might be going extinct. I'm also being trained on animals that are having the same thing happen to them." Aaron stopped circling the couch to look at Jake. "I have no idea why I just told you that. I'm to keep it a secret so that I'm not killed or taken captive by one of the groups that think we're messing with nature. Perhaps we are, but there isn't any reason to think that we can't help some things along when they need it."

"I would never betray a confidence, Aaron. But do you think that Brody will be one of those people?" Aaron told him no, he didn't for some reason. "I don't either. I do think, however, that he'd be helpful in your job. Him being a doctor would lend you information that you might otherwise not have."

"I've thought of that too when my head wasn't ready to pop off." They both laughed and Aaron felt better for it. "I'm sounding like someone that is a homophobic. I'm not. I don't want you to think that of me."

"I don't. You're confused." He said he was very confused. "Believe me when I tell you that it gets better. And Forrest helped me to understand the same things that you're thinking. I was a married man with a home and money. The feelings that came to me when I met Forrest were as alien to me as yours for Brody. Lucky for me, I guess, Forrest was comfortable with his life. And after a while, about ten minutes of being with him, I was as well. It's actually liberating to know that it wasn't all me when it came to satisfying women when it came to sex. Believe me, I tried to with my wife. But after a while, I simply didn't care if either of us were happy. Which, we were not."

59

"I haven't any idea where to go from here. Honestly, I feel something when I'm with Brody. Comfort, for one thing. I'm safe is another. And when I'm sitting with him, I feel as if everything that I'm thinking about doing at the time is meaningless with him by my side." He looked at Jake. "I sound like I'm waxing poetic, don't I? Or trying to justify this for some reason. No, not justify. I mean, I'm trying to come to terms with this. Yes, that's it. Coming to...holy shit, Jake. I really want to be with Brody. Do you think he'll want to be with me too?"

"I would, yes." Aaron turned to look toward the doorway, and saw not only Brody there, but also Forrest. When he and Jake left, Brody came to sit with him. It was just like he'd said — he was safe. His mind ordered itself and he was happy. "We should get to know each other. I mean, other than through sex, which I will admit, is all I've thought about for the last couple of hours."

"Me too." Aaron relaxed by degrees. He felt like he could talk now. Perhaps not about sex — as Brody had said, they shouldn't right now — but other things in his life. "I'd very much like to get to know you a bit better. And your family. I already love your son to pieces. And I know that Emmi and he have a special bond too."

"If you call her getting tackled at the airport with him a bond, then yes, I'd say they do." He and Brody laughed. "I'm in the process of getting a divorce. You might have heard that. I came here with the intention of starting new and opening a clinic or offices here. But since being here, I've been asked to work at the hospital, as well as being the police physician. That, I have to tell you, has been my dream my entire life."

"Then go for it." Brody shook his head. "Why not? I mean, when an opportunity falls in your lap that you'd like to do, then do it. If it turns out that it wasn't the job you'd thought it would be, change again. It's how I ended up working for the government on the wildlife preservation committee."

"I know what that is. That's an amazing job. To preserve species and to help them along when they're close to extinction—how fulfilling will that be someday when you're looking at a species that might have been gone without your help? I love that. And thank you." His excitement was perfect, and just what Aaron needed. "I bet you have to travel a bit."

Brody got up and moved to the door, and Aaron thought for sure that he was just going to leave him there. His heart felt like he'd taken a hard blow to it. His mind went back to feeling inadequate. He didn't know where that feeling came from, but—

"Aren't you hungry?" Aaron nodded at Brody's question. "Well, come on. Howie just yelled for us to come. You must not have heard him. I know he's a bit unorthodox, but he's my friend as well as—"

Aaron stopped Brody from babbling with his mouth. The kiss was a little hard and awkward, but he just wanted to touch him in a different way, one that made him feel like he was his. Aaron stepped back and looked at Brody when the kiss ended.

"I think we can do better than that, don't you?" Aaron felt like a small boy getting a big treat for doing something. Again, the thought came out of left field, but when Brody pulled him in for a kiss, again it was awkward, but they figured it out and kissed like they needed.

It wasn't like kissing a woman, Aaron thought. It was more. It was better. This time when they pulled apart they were both breathing hard, and this time he did hear Howie yell for them from the kitchen.

"That was...that was amazing." He laughed. Aaron was so relieved that he didn't know he'd been holding his breath all that time. "I would still like to get to know you, but taking this one step at a time, I think we can make it work out better for the both of us. Plus, I need to talk to my son."

They went into the kitchen separately. They both knew that Jordan was in there. So was the rest of the household. Aaron understood the reason for this, and he was all right with it. He and Brody were a couple, and that was perfect.

"I've been thinking about you two." Aaron felt his face heat up as Jake spoke, looking down at Jordan. Jake nodded as he continued. "With the divorce proceeding the way it is, I think that as you two get to know each other and your working schedules, your personal life should be on the downlow. At least until this thing is over. And you'll be happy to know that the books that your father told you about, Brody, are just what we needed to end this reasonably."

"Do you believe that it'll work that way?" Forrest told Brody that he didn't, but it would end with him getting Jordan. Jordan was never one to miss an opportunity to whoop it up, Aaron had come to realize, and he did so at top decimals. "I take it you two have come to terms?"

"I think so. We're going slowly."

Paddy burst in the back door, as loud if not louder than Jordan had been. "It's there. Look. My book has been out for four hours, and it's already on the bestseller list. I mean, it's ninety-four, but it's on the fucking list." Paddy looked at Jordan and said he was sorry.

"Don't worry about it, Uncle Paddy, I've heard it all before. My mom is a slut too." Jordan left them then, and Brody looked at his mom. Aaron didn't know if he was struggling with his anger or laughter. It could have been either.

"I might have said that out loud." Williemae flushed brightly. "All right, I said it a few times. That woman is going to be the death of us all, I tell you. But I will try and refrain from saying it so much in front of Jordan. I'll try, Brody."

"I guess that's all I can ask for." Big subs were set in front of both of them. The others were already eating. "If you keep cooking like this, Howie, I might have to have a gym membership again."

"You'll burn it off." It just slipped out, and even Aaron was shocked at what he'd said. "I'm so sorry." But when they laughed, all of them, he shook his head and began to eat.

Aaron was happy, he realized. And for the first time in his life. Before today, he'd thought himself happy about a few things in his life. But this, with Brody and his family, his sister nearby and hopefully happy too, things couldn't get any better. Now they just had to finish up a few things and they'd be on their way to more happiness.

Then his cell rang at almost the same time as Brody's. Brody had an emergency at the hospital, and Aaron was being called out on an assignment. They had located an animal that they'd thought was gone. Excited for everything now, he drove himself to the airport and Brody drove to the hospital. Yes, Aaron thought, it was nice to finally feel good about life.

# *Chapter 5*

Jordan was having a good time with Emmi. She was so funny sometimes that he forgot that they were shopping. Normally he didn't care for shopping for anything, but he had outgrown all his clothes and needed some pants for the cooler months. He heard Emmi sigh for the second time.

"You don't have to do this. I can wait for my dad." She looked at him with so much hope in her eyes that he was disappointed. "Really, it's all right, Emmi, I can find some later."

"No. I really want to do this. But I know shit about buying clothing for a five-year-old. I mean, do you want to look cool? Is that something that we should be working on? And once you try them on what do I do?"

"I'll show you when I try these on." He went to the little changing room and started to undress. He heard Emmi talking and realized that she was speaking to him.

"Hey, Kid, you in there?" She was forever calling him kid. Jordan kind of liked it. He told her he was fine. "I have this shirt here that I like. I mean, if you don't, then we can put it back. Will you try it on?"

"Sure." He knew that he'd pick it out to take home even if it was ugly. Emmi had found him something that she liked. As soon as she tossed it under the half door, Jordan knew that he was going to love it. "Emmi, this is so soft. And I love the color."

Jordan pulled it over his head and looked at himself in the mirror. It was nice, and he thought that the color was just like Emmi's eyes—so green that it almost hurt to see it move on his body. Coming out of the little room, he asked her how it looked.

"Christ, Kid. You look like a model or something. Now, show me how your dad figures out if your pants fit." He laughed when she told him how she figured hers out. "If they don't pinch me or fall off, I buy them."

"I don't know why, but he jerks them around here." He showed her on his hips with the pants. "Then he tugs on the legs. I never know if he's trying to stretch the pants or he just likes to do that. But that's what he does. And don't ask me if it works. All I know is that sometimes he lets me get them, other times he tells me they don't fit."

She jerked him around by his pants until he fell to the floor. They were both laughing when he looked over Emmi's shoulder. His entire body froze up and he didn't know what to do. Jordan was afraid that he was going to wet his pants. His mom was there.

"What the hell are you doing with my son?" Emmi whispered in his ear to go into the dressing room and to lock the door. "I asked you a question, bitch. Give him to me now and I won't make a scene. And if you have any money to buy his things, I'll take that too. I'll buy my own son his clothing, thank you very much."

Jordan was five and a kid. As much as he wanted to protect Emmi, he knew that his mom would hurt him, and then his new aunt. Hiding under the bench that was in the room with him, he pulled all the clothing towards him and touched the cell phone that Aaron had given him this morning.

There were a bunch of numbers in it, he'd been told, and on the back someone had printed a list of who each number would dial. Speed dial was what he needed right now. Thinking about who to call, he touched his fingers to the one that was for Henry.

"Whatcha need, Jordan?" He told him in a whisper what was going on. "I'll be there in a moment. Just you sit tight. Emmi is much stronger than she looks. Just hold on, buddy. Paddy and I are in the mall now, and will be there soon."

Jordan screamed when the door opened. He felt stupid when it was just Emmi and she smiled at him, coming into where he was to sit on the floor. Coming out from under the bench and clothing, he hugged Emmi tightly when she told him his mom was gone.

"I thought for sure we were both dead. I'm so glad that you didn't get hurt. Did you kill her? I hope so. I know that's not nice, but I don't care about her anymore. I love you and the rest of the family that took us in. And I've had so much fun shopping with you, I'd like to do—"

"Jordan." He snapped his mouth closed hard enough to hurt his teeth when Emmi said his name. "I didn't kill her. Though it was tempting. I called the police and they'll be here soon, so you just wait for them, all right?"

"Yes." He hugged her again, telling her that he'd called Henry. "I didn't know what she would do to you, and I love you too much for you to get hurt."

"I love you too, Kid. You're sort of growing on me. Like a fungus." She made him laugh and Jordan felt better for it. "Now, this is what we're going to do before anyone comes. You redress in your clothing and we'll pay for what you want. All right? I don't want to even be in this store anymore. Do you?"

"No. It's tainted." She looked at him with a cocked head. "I'm not a dummy just because I'm a kid, you know."

"I'm beginning to see that." Emmi hugged him again and started out the door. Jordan asked her not to go too far. "I won't, Kid. I'll be right here. But we are going to get you a couple more of those shirts, in different styles and colors. Those are nice."

He ended up getting two pair of pants and four shirts, two of which were the soft ones. As they were paying up, the police arrived and mostly Emmi, who was working off and on as a police officer when they were short, spoke to them. Then Henry and Paddy showed up. Cattie, Cam's sister, was one of the police officers with them, and she made sure he was unharmed too.

The police didn't stick around long. Jordan was glad. He wasn't stressed out anymore, but now he was starving. When he asked if they could get something to eat, they all said they were hungry too. Jordan felt like the king of the world then. Emmi sat on one side of him, Cattie on the other. Jordan decided that he'd like to marry one of them someday, but he knew he was just a kid. But he'd grow up and they'd like him more, he thought.

"Hey, Kid. I have a serious question for you." He looked at Cattie when she called him kid too. He knew that she'd caught him a couple of times watching Paddy and Henry. They held hands a great deal and kissed a lot. Jordan wondered if he was in trouble for staring. Mom would have gone to them and told them off; Jordan had seen her do it. "What do you know about homosexual couples? Anything that's not mean?"

"No. My mom, she was really mean to them. Terrible mean, and she'd call them names too." He looked at Paddy and Henry. "They are, I think. And they sure do love each other. And I think that Jake and Forrest are too. I wish my dad could find someone that loved him like that. He sure would be happy."

Jordan wasn't sure that he meant for his dad to be a homosexual or not. Not that it mattered to him. All he wanted in the world was his mom gone and his dad to be happy. Like these people were.

Letting the conversation flow around him, he thought of Aaron. He'd had a long conversation with him just before he'd left today. Jordan had never had anyone talk to him like that before. Man to man, Aaron called it, and told him that he'd be back soon.

"You keep an eye on your dad for me. With your mom around, I don't want anything to happen to either of you. And sometimes your dad forgets that he doesn't have to be looking over his shoulder all the time and forgets to have fun. Understand?" Jordan asked if it was because of his mom. "Mostly, yes. But he worries for you too. And your grandma and Howie. I want you to make him have a little fun too. Watch a movie with him. Even toss popcorn at him. Just make him smile and forget that your loony mom is out to get him."

He had promised him he would, then Aaron had hugged him. It was a strange feeling, to be hugged so wonderfully by someone that he didn't know all that well. But he had hugged him back.

Jordan wondered if Aaron and dad holding hands meant that his dad was a homosexual too. Thoughts of his dad and Aaron filtered through his head. He wondered if they'd love each other and forget about him. His mom had when she'd found that Ralph guy. And she'd hurt him, smacking him around just to make Ralph laugh with her.

He was trying on a shirt in another store when Emmi said

his name again, softly.

"What gives, Kid? You thinking that you've had enough shopping for one day? If so, then I'm disappointed. I wanted to get this done so we could maybe have some homemade cookies at the store before we went home."

"Is my dad gay?" Emmi didn't look around like she was embarrassed by the question, but asked him why he thought that. "I saw him holding hands with Aaron. And they hugged a lot today. Are they going to forget about me too?"

He started crying and Emmi held him. No one stared at them. And no one made fun of him for being such a big baby. Jordan just held onto Emmi like she was his rope in the deep end of the pool. She was saving him.

"All right. You done sobbing all over my new shirt, Kid?" He nodded and looked up at her. She handed him a tissue and he wiped his face. "First of all, would it bother you to know that he is? And that he and Aaron are going to be a couple like the others? Before you answer that, I want you to know that I talked to Aaron earlier, as well as your dad when he had a minute. They said if you were to ask questions, I could answer them for you, but you were to understand that they were both going to talk to you when they were home again. All right?"

"Heck no, it wouldn't bother me. Are you nuts? The rest of them are so happy, it makes me happy. And they sure do know how to have fun too. My dad forgot how to do that, I think." Emmi nodded. "I saw them holding hands at home. I didn't care. I still don't, but I don't want them to forget me."

"Why do you think that if they're a couple they'd forget you? I mean, I've tried to forget you daily, and you're like that fungus I was telling you about earlier. You have sort of grown on me." He told her what he'd been thinking about Ralph and his mom. "Okay, think about who you're comparing your dad to. That is not a role model that I'd want to compare anyone to. She's a nutball, and more than likely hasn't loved anyone in her life. And as much as it pains me to say it, probably not you either."

"She said she didn't love me. I was just her ticket. I had to ask Grandma what that meant, and she told me that Mom wanted to get more money out of Dad." Emmi asked if it worked. "I don't know, dork, I wasn't born yet."

Emmi tickled him again, and he started to stand up to hug her. But she had him pause, she told him, until she figured this out. He waited, not sure what she was talking about until she snapped her fingers. Nothing changed, but she was happy about it. He asked her what had happened. She got down to his level before answering.

"Did you know that Quincey is my mate?" He nodded. "Well, he's given me some of his powers because we're mates. So, in answer to your question, I pulled shadows around us just now so that no one would see or hear us while you were upset. I just didn't remember how to make it go away. We'd have had a hard time paying for things if no one could see us."

"Yeah. That would be funny though. But you and Quincey, wow, that's so good for you. You were so sad when I saw you the first time. That's why I thought I could trust you. You looked like you'd been hurt enough, and that you'd not hurt me." Emmi hugged him tightly, and he wasn't sure she was going to let him go. And when she did, he looked at her. "I love you, Emmi. Very much. And if you don't care, I'd like to call you my aunt too. You are the best person I know in the world."

"I'd be honored to have you call me Aunt Emmi."

They finished up shopping just as his dad joined them. She told him about his mom, and then told them both what she'd done to make her go away.

"I made her think that she'd been mistaken about me having Jordan and that she should go home. I should have made her go to the police, but I wasn't sure how to do that part. I'm still learning a lot of things, but that one I'm getting better at. I've sort of gotten a crash course in everything vampire in the last two days."

After transferring his bags to Dad's car, they headed home. Jordan was tired, but he wanted to spend some time with his dad. Do what Aaron had asked him to do—make him happy. As they were taking all his bags up to his room, Dad asked him if he'd had fun.

"I did." Taking a deep breath, he let it out slowly. "Dad, are you and Aaron going to be sleeping together? Like the rest of them are?"

~*~

Brody sat down on the bed, thankful that it was there so he'd not hit the floor. All day, while he was putting a man's face back together who'd tangled with his wife who had an electric knife, he'd thought of very little but Jordan.

"Why do you ask? Did someone say something to you? By the way, I know that you talked to Emmi and the others. But how did you know that Aaron and I were together?" Jordan sat down at his desk. It, like the rest of his room, was covered in clothing that either didn't fit or wouldn't by winter. Brody picked up a shirt to fold it. "I need to know what you've heard so that I can go from there."

"Nobody said anything. Not really. Emmi asked me some questions about me knowing anything about it, and she did ask me if it would bother me if you were like them. It doesn't. Not at all. But I was with Paddy and Henry today at the mall. And they seem to be really happy. I want you to be happy. You never was with Mom, I don't think." Brody's mind screamed at him to deny it, but his heart told him this was a good opening for him to talk. "Dad, are you mad at me for asking you?"

"No. Goodness no. I just don't want to mess up here. You're my son, and above anything else, I want you to be happy too." Jordan told him he was. "Good. Good. That's good."

"Dad, just tell me. You're making me nervous." Brody thought that his nervousness couldn't be worse than his was at the moment. "Dad?"

"Yes, Aaron and I are going to be a couple. We are a couple." Jordan nodded as Brody let out a long breath. He sat down again before his trembling legs gave out on him. "But we're doing this slowly. For all of us, including you. And we can't have your mom figuring it out either. We're not embarrassed about it, but she isn't a nice person, and she'll make sure that I have a black mark against us. She'll have grounds to take you if we tell anyone just yet. Rachel will say that the home isn't stable or something like that. I don't want you to lie, Jordan. But don't make a big deal out of it, all right?"

"I won't, Dad, I promise. I don't want to go with her. I want to stay here with you and Aaron. And Grandma and Howie. Aunt Emmi said I could go to her studio when she gets it set up. And she's going to come and see about painting something on my walls for me." Jordan laughed. "She said she was going to come over and paint some—well, poop, but that's not what she said. I asked; she's not really painting poop on my walls."

"Thank God." Brody laughed with his son. "Jordan, this is really important. You understand that, don't you? A lot of people in this world don't like gay people. They think that they're deviants and other things that aren't true. But they're not—we're not. We're just people, like everyone else. So you be extra careful who you tell and say anything in front of. All right, son?"

"Yes." He looked around his room, then back at him. "Dad, will you forget about me? I don't mean forget, but leave me alone and stuff when you go out with Aaron? Aunt Emmi said you won't, but I don't know. That's what Mom did when she found that guy, Ralph. She shoved me aside like old shoes with holes in them. Grandma told me that one. I think she's a hoot, don't you?"

Brody got up and picked his son up in his arms. He'd forgotten that he was so big. He supposed he should have had a clue, what with the clothing that no longer fit him. Brody was startled by his height and weight. Jordan was growing up, and getting smarter every day along with it.

"I would never ever forget you. Neither will Aaron. He worries about you as much as I do, Jordan. He told me that when he gets back from this assignment, he wants to figure out what you like to do so he can be a part of both our lives." Jordan didn't look convinced. "I swear to you, Jordan. Forever you will be the first thing in my life. Aaron will have to be second, because you have so much of my heart that he will have to wait in line, so far as I'm concerned. He makes me happy, and I probably love him, but I do love you and will forever. You might not be a part of me, Jordan, but you certainly hold my heart. Do you understand me, son?"

"Yes. I love you, Dad."

Setting Jordan on the floor when he seemed to want to be let go, Brody helped him gather up his room. The first thing they did together was to put all the clothing that he was no longer able to wear in neat stacks on the bed. Then he opened the shopping bags. "What did the two of you do, buy out the store?"

74

He showed him the beautiful shirts, and it occurred to Brody that Jordan had a crush on Emmi. Sure that he'd bought them because she had liked them, he asked him to try one on. He did so without hesitation.

"It's very soft and warm. I bet that I never have to wear a coat again with this one. I have two of them too." He asked if they'd gotten him a coat. "Yeah. Aunt Emmi got her one too. Though after she got it, she figured that she'd not need it with her being part vampire and all."

His son seemed to be more comfortable with all this than he was. Which, he supposed, was about right. Jordan had been at the pack house where things were very different than at a regular school. And he'd been told that kids from a lot of different walks of life went there, mostly for safety reasons. But he also thought that him being a child helped too. Children, he'd figured out, were much more accepting than adults could be.

Jordan could also do more on his computer than Brody could. Then there was the remote to the television. Brody would struggle for ten minutes before he'd have to hand it over to Jordan, who would take less than a second to get them on the correct channel. Brody watched, fascinated, as Jordan pulled up Emmi on his cell phone and talked to her on the speaker.

"Dad really likes the stuff we got." Emmi told them both that she'd had a good time. "Me too. And I told Dad that you would have me over to your studio as soon as you got it set up too."

"I'm actually almost done. Hang on and let me show you it this way first." The phone turned and he saw the paints on shelves, as well as the canvas, in different sizes, lined up against the wall. "I don't have anything painted here yet, but my other work is on its way from my old apartment. I forgot to let you know where our house is. Remember what I told you about it, Jordan?"

"Yes, you said that a vampire's lair is like their special place. No one enters unless they for sure want to die, and anyone who is invited is trustworthy and a friend." Brody was impressed, with both of them. "We have to have dinner, then watch a movie later. Do you and Quincey want to come over and join us? We're having burgers and French fries." Brody laughed when Emmi told him that asking his dad first might be good. Jordan looked at him.

"Yes, please come over. Aaron is out of the country until sometime tomorrow, and we're just the two of us until they all return. Mom and Howie went out to dinner." She asked if Jake and the rest were coming over, and this time Brody looked at Jordan. When he agreed, Brody laughed. "Why not? I don't know how much hamburger we have, but we'll think of something."

"And sometime soon, very soon, we all need to get a taste of you. Just so we can find you. Quincey only needs scent, I guess, but since I'm not up people's asses all the time for a scent, I need to bite you." She wiggled her brows and they both laughed. "We'll see you guys in about a half an hour. I'll let the rest of them know too."

By the time Brody and Jordan figured out that they didn't have nearly enough food for them, everyone was piling into the kitchen. Apparently, they had stopped at the local market on the way in. There were bags upon bags of food everywhere. Most of it was pre-made, as few of them really cooked, but he was fine with it. He wasn't alone in his life anymore. Brody had friends.

Paddy and Christy were at the grill. Quincey was filling glasses with ice and pouring tea for everyone. There was potato salad, macaroni salad, chips, as well as pickles and other condiments. He was just pulling out plates that had only arrived today when Jordan came into the dining room with his computer. Before he could tell him no electronics at mealtime, he saw Aaron on the screen.

"Hello everyone." They all cheered and Brody had to sit down as Aaron told them he was glad to see them. "I'm having good luck today, so I should be home sometime after midnight. Tomorrow morning at the latest. I forgot to extend my stay at the hotel there in town, so I'm hoping that I have a place to stay since Emmi moved out of her apartment and gave it up."

Everyone turned to Brody and he felt his face heat up. But before he could say anything, like come here, Jordan spoke first.

"Come here, Uncle Aaron. We have lots of bedrooms, and the towels came today too. Dad will probably wait up for you, so you don't even have to have a key." Jordan looked at him and winked. Brody burst out laughing. "I just thought this would be fun for everyone since Uncle Aaron told me his phone number before he left, and with us all here and he's not, we could just talk to him."

"It was perfect, Jordan. I was just thinking about all of you anyway, and how much I missed you guys." He looked to his right, then said something in another language before looking back at the camera he had on his end. "I have to get going. But if it's all right with you, Brody, it would make me feel good to come there."

"I would like that too. And Jordan has a list of things he needs to ask you as well." Aaron laughed and said he'd be home soon. "Bye, and I'm so glad we all got to see you."

The rest of the night was a blur of fun and laughter. But most importantly, getting acquainted with each other. Brody ate too much food, and when the pies were brought out, he groaned but ate two pieces of peach anyway. Clean up was an affair as well. Everyone, like when they were cooking dinner, did their part with taking on a task. Conversation was light and fun. They didn't bring up the divorce, nor the relationship between he and Aaron, but just about everything else under the sun was fair game.

At nine, when everyone was leaving, Jordan went up to his bed with the biggest smile on his face. He was almost asleep as Brody was tucking him in. And when he kissed him good night, he held him a little longer than usual. His little boy was growing up, too fast, Brody thought. It was only a matter of time, he realized, before Jordan went to middle school, then high school. Before Brody knew it, he'd be off to college. Laughing at himself as he made his way down the stairs, he wondered when he'd gotten all melancholy and gloomy.

Setting himself up to wait for Aaron to come home, he watched a movie. There had been too much food from earlier and he was still stuffed. But he found himself in the kitchen making popcorn. He was making fun of himself when his phone went off—the guard house.

"Dr. Downs. I know that you and Mr. Wright know each other, but I wanted to make sure that he's welcome at this time of night." He thought about what to say. "If he's going to be a regular, then I can just pass him through from now on."

"Yes, he's going to be living here too." Mr. Taylor said that was good, and he heard him wave Aaron on through. "Mr. Taylor, you've not seen my ex-wife around, have you? I don't want you hurt either."

"Nope, not a peep from her. But I will tell you, Dr. Downs, she won't get past me unless I'm dead. And if she gets to you, then you got her for trespassing. Don't waste no time talking to her either. You just blow her fucking head off." He didn't want to think of this man hurt because of Rachel. "I'm just like you, Dr. Downs. An immortal. So unless she gets a head shot in and it sticks, I'm going to be just fine."

Brody thanked him and started to the front door. Then what he'd said hit him. Immortal? He wasn't immortal. Was he? Tonight he'd exchanged blood with all the shifters and vampires that had come by, and allowed Jordan to do the same. But an immortal?

As soon as he heard the knock at the door, all thoughts of living forever flew out of his mind. Aaron was home. Aaron was here now. Opening the door, he stepped aside as Aaron entered and asked where Jordan was.

"He has school tomorrow, so he's in bed."

No sooner had he said that than Brody found himself on his back on the floor, with Aaron tearing at his clothing.

"So much for waiting."

They were both laughing as they touched each other.

# Chapter 6

Aaron didn't know what would be too much for Brody, but for himself, he was totally and completely overwhelmed. Rolling to his back, he let the coolness of the tile beneath him cool off his body. Brody rolled too, but to his side, and looked at him. It was then that he realized that his shirt was torn up and his belt was undone.

"We should go upstairs." Aaron nodded but didn't move. Neither of them did. "I want to sleep with you. Very much so. But I don't know if I'm ready for sex at the moment. I will more than likely change my mind as soon as we get up there, but for now, I just want to be held by you."

"That sounds perfect." Aaron stood up and helped Brody. They were headed to the stairs when he looked at him. "I'm guessing that you had a talk with Jordan. That kid is smart, Brody. We have to get him into some computer classes to help him along."

"You're right, he is, and I think he's helping with the computer classes at the pack school. They love him there. About us? Actually, he had a talk with me. I guess he'd been thinking about the other couples, and was worried that once you and I got together that we'd forget about him. I was going to talk to you about that. We need to make sure we include him in a lot of our day to day things." Aaron said he was thinking the same thing. He loved Jordan. "When this is all over—I don't know how it will work other than to have you as his guardian too—but I'd like for you to have just as much say about him as I do. That way, if I'm working and can't get away, you can made decisions for him as well."

"Good idea." They were at the top of the landing when they both stopped for a moment. "So, I can move into your room? Or should I have my stuff in one of the other bedrooms? To me, that makes sense. As Jake said, we can't give her anything she can use to get our son."

When he didn't correct him, Aaron reached for Brody's hand. It was a little too much right now. Neither of them had had a clue that they had been with the wrong sex all their lives. And Aaron, while he was away, had thought about his life around women.

"When I was seventeen, this girl I knew in college took me to her room and did all kinds of things to my body. She never let me come, nor actually have sex, but my God, I spent the next week, until she came home again, with a raging hard on." They were in the bedroom now. "I remember thinking when I finally did have sex with her—or I should say, came all over her—it wasn't all that satisfying. Not that, like I said, I didn't come. But it was more of just a release than actually having a climax."

Aaron was naked before Brody. He didn't own any pajamas, and wasn't sure what to do about it. But when Brody got into bed in the buff, he joined him. The two of them laid there for several minutes until Brody spoke.

"My first disappointment with sex was with Rachel. She had way more experience than I did. But like you, it wasn't all that satisfying. Anyway, it was our wedding night, and I was like a teen virgin, hard as stone and waiting for my new wife to come out and have sex with me." Brody turned to him. "That's all I've ever had with women. Sex. There wasn't any making love. Nothing about it that made me think that this was it, the thing that all men want. Anyway, our wedding night was about to happen, and when she came out of the bathroom I just stared at her."

"What happened?" Brody moved closer to him, his body warmed by the blanket. When Aaron spooned in so that Brody was in front of him, his back to Aaron's chest, Aaron felt his cock stretch, his entire body harden. "What happened?"

"I laughed." Aaron stopped moving, his body rocking into Brody's by its own volition. "I laughed hard, too. I mean, I fell to the floor, breaking the champagne glass that was in my hand. Knocking over the nice basket of fruit and shit that my partners had sent. I mean, I was almost drunk with laughter. And as you can imagine, she wasn't the least bit happy with it."

"What was so funny? I mean, sure you found out later that you're a homo, but what was so fucking funny that you laughed at your new wife?"

Brody was still laughing, like he was remembering it so fondly that he just couldn't help himself. And soon, Aaron was joining him.

"She had toilet paper stuck to her foot." Now they both were laughing so hard that they were crying. He could see it now, a woman dressed up in her sexiest nighty, to no doubt impress her new husband, and she had a long trail of toilet paper dragging out from the floor. "And you know what? It was still on the roll. So when she came at me to hit me for laughing, the roll of paper emptied, and there she was with her white train again, like it was her veil or something."

It took them another hour to calm down. Both of them would snicker or something when they were remaking the bed. They'd laughed so hard Brody had fallen out of the bed, and when he'd tried to help him up, Aaron had brought all the blankets with him. Brody confessed that he'd never told anyone that before.

"I'm glad you shared it with me. I think that it was something that we both needed. But I have to ask, did she let you have sex with her after that?"

Brody laughed and shook his head. "She even acted like I should have been sorrier than I was about laughing and not getting to fuck her." They got into bed and cuddled again. "I'm glad that you're here. With us. I just don't think I would have been feeling like I am right now without you by my side."

He and Brody talked for the rest of the night. Nothing earthshattering, just getting to know each other. He knew a great many things about his mate, and he'd told him a lot about himself. They were friends now—better than friends, they were going to be lovers who were not going into this without being close first. Of course he had a raging hard on, and he knew that Brody did as well. But it was all right. They were all right. They'd just have to take a lot of cold showers, that was all.

Closing his eyes, Aaron let sleep roll over him. He was exhausted. Holding Brody made him feel good, and sleep had never been so easy to slide into than it was this night.

~*~

Waking to a dark room, Brody wasn't sure what had happened. He was alone, that much he'd figured out, and when he was reaching for something to pull on, he heard Aaron speak nearby.

"Don't turn on the lights." He said all right. "Come to the

window. I want you to see this. It's beautiful. Just don't move fast."

He got to the window and was thankful for the bright moon. There on the lawn were two wolves and a small cub, playing in the new fallen snow. It wasn't deep yet, barely an inch, and would more than likely be gone when the sun came up. However, the wolves, the family of them, were having a wonderful time.

"I got up because I had a terrible cramp." Brody asked him where it was, and Aaron touched his ass with his cock. "Sorry. I'm so hard that I can barely breathe through it."

Brody reached behind him just enough to wrap his hand around Aaron's cock, and they both moaned. Sliding his hand up and down his shaft, Brody turned when Aaron reached for his as well. They were both enjoying what they were doing, and when Aaron kissed him on his shoulder, then his neck, Brody turned into his body and touched his free hand to Aarons chest.

His nipples were hard as stone. The soft fur that covered his chest was thick. Running his fingers through it, Brody leaned in and took his nipple into his mouth and suckled it hard. When he bit down on it, not too hard, Aaron cried out.

"I need more. I need you." Lying on the bed, neither of them were sure what to do. "I want to touch you. Everywhere. Then I want to take your cock in my mouth until you come."

Brody nearly did come then, especially when Aaron touched him. It didn't even matter that it was only his arm. It sent waves of electrical pulses throughout his entire body. When Aaron rolled over him to sit on his knees between Brody's legs, Brody watched as Aaron did a sort of peep show for him by touching his own body.

His hands rubbed his chest, pausing long enough to play with his nipples. His cock was straining hard, but he never touched himself there. Cupping his own balls, Brody's mouth watered, his shaft strained. Looking down at their cocks, so close together, Brody wasn't surprised by the amount of pre-cum dripping from the tip of them both. Leaning up enough to touch his finger to Aaron's, he put the warm juices into his mouth.

"Christ, yes."

Aaron moved off the bed. Brody wasn't sure what to do until Aaron put his mouth over his member. Brody wanted to scream, to beg him to stop, yet he needed more. And when Aaron swallowed him down, the tightness of his throat muscles was like a strangling force and just what he needed to come.

Nothing could have prepared him for the climax that he had. Never in all his thoughts about being with this man had he thought that sex would do this to him—knock his eyes to the back of his head, make his body feel like it had been turned inside out and then slammed back the right way. Reaching down to pull Aaron from his cock, he felt his balls being abused, and when they were twisted in an amazing way, he came again.

It was just as fulfilling, just as life altering. And when he reached for Aaron this time, he came to him willingly, letting go of his cock like it had been the hardest thing he'd ever done. Brody was sure it was—he never wanted to let this man go, ever.

Taking Aaron's cock into his mouth, Brody took his time. He had less urgency, no less of a need, but he was more in control. But Aaron wasn't. He needed. There wasn't any reason to say what he needed either. It was written all over his face, much like he was sure his own face looked.

"Please. I need you to give me relief before I die."

He watched Aaron as he went lower on his cock. When

he cupped his balls in his hand, Brody couldn't believe how hot they were, how heavy. And when he turned them, not sure if he was going to hurt him, Brody got his first taste of the most amazing elixir that he could have ever dreamed of.

Aaron came so hard that Brody nearly couldn't keep up with him. Crying out when he came a second time, Brody thought for sure they were both going to wake the house. Standing up, begging him for a moment, Brody wrapped his hand around his own cock and felt the need, incredibly, to come again.

He and Aaron slid their hands up and town each others' shafts. Not too quickly, as he had been relieved, and so had Aaron. But when Aaron said he was coming, his body bent up from the bed, Brody came as soon as his partner did, his love's cum sprayed over his chest and face.

The room darkened for a moment. Brody fell atop Aaron, his legs simply unable to hold up his weight any longer. Crawling over the other man, he made his way to the top of the bed and collapsed. If Aaron moved or even got to the pillow, Brody had no idea. And as much as he wanted to check on him, he just couldn't move. Sleep took him like he'd been given a sedative. He was simply out.

~*~

Fred tried to figure out where the girl had gone. She always slipped into the store on her way home from going to the gallery once a week. Fred would make sure he followed her close enough to put the drugs on her food. Somedays it worked well; others, he had to keep an eye on her. If she didn't eat the tainted food right away, then it became a game for them — one he always won.

She was easy pickings, Emmi was. Emmi Wright was stupid. To Fred, he supposed everyone was. And so far, after all these years of making a killing off these poor, lonely, stupid people, he had never come up empty handed or put in jail. He was careful, and smart.

Walking around the little store, he tried to make himself look like he was shopping. Fred didn't eat this sort of food. Who in their right mind would have a salad and fruit when there was meat, beef, pork, chicken, and a plethora of other creatures that were slaughtered just for one's plate?

He saw his next woman. She was skinny, and her cart was filled with things that only someone that lived alone would buy. A single frozen dinner. A single can of soup. Fred wondered if any of these pieces of ass ever realized how much they gave away by what they brought home.

Not that he had sex with them. No, that could get a person into more trouble than it was worth. Condoms would hide most of the DNA, but there were things like sweat and pubic hairs that could get you killed. He never touched their bodies if he could help it. The instruments that he used were cleaned and soaked in bleach every time he used them. The perfect crime.

And he'd perfected it. There had always been a saying, "There is no such thing as a perfect crime." Bullshit. He knew better. Fred had been doing it for years upon years. But he couldn't tell anyone. That would get him caught sure as shit.

When his "date" didn't show again, he decided it was time to go by her house. He needed a little action, and the fact that she was taking it from him sort of pissed him off. But, he knew, an angry person was a risky one.

The woman that he'd picked out was standing in the line at the grocery checkout. She even did him a favor by going to one of the self-checkout places. Watching her carefully, so as not to startle her, he nearly fell into her cart—part of his ploy—and dropped the little drops of drugs on top of her open bag of salad makings. No one was the wiser when he made his way out of the store and took off his wig and heavy fat coat.

Fred knew about cameras being hidden in places where you couldn't see them. He also knew that if someone happened to see him use his tool, then they'd be looking for a fat man with gray hair. He changed his costume so often that there were times when they put out a picture of him, even he didn't know if it was him or some other person. Fred was that damned good.

He waited in his car. That was another thing that he did — changed his car like he did his costumes. There wasn't any way that he'd be caught because he owned this or that car. He didn't own any. But his women did. Emmi, for instance, owned two cars that he used to drive around, an apartment in New York, as well several hundred thousand dollars in credit cards she'd given over to him.

Not really, he told himself. But he had had a good time going through her trash and finding the invitations, then calling them to have a new credit card in her name. For most people he targeted, the amount they'd get was very low. But he didn't use it wisely. Why should he?

But with little Emmi, she must have had some stellar credit, because the first time he cashed in on one of the offers, he was able to get a hundred grand with low interest for eighteen months. He hadn't told her about the timeline, but had used up the credit on a vacation, and of course, the apartment in New York.

He'd never been to it. Never even been to New York, as a matter of fact. But he'd seen it for sale in the paper and had jumped right on it. And she was making the monthly payments on it, because he'd checked. She was good for a few more thousand dollars, too.

But he got the most thrills in beating the shit out of her.

KATHI S. BARTON

Well, not just her, but any woman that he decided would be good for him and a few bucks. She would fight back—even while on the drugs he'd given her to make her fall into a deep sleep, she'd fight back. There were a couple of times that he was glad that he'd worn a facemask—Emmi had come that close to cutting him with her nails. And that wouldn't do.

Fred would kill any of the women if they touched him. They'd disappear like a fart in the wind. He'd break their little neck then take them to his hideaway. There, he not only had the means to get rid of the body, but it was also the place where he stored his car collection.

No one knew where he stored his collection, as he called it. The cars, and other things that the women had, he'd put in the storage containers that his dad had collected over the years before his death.

Dad's plan had been to build a house by putting all the containers either side by side or on top of each other. He even had all the windows that he was going to put in. The windows he'd gotten from houses that were being torn down, and were covered in so much dirt and grime now, you couldn't tell if they were glass or just a part of the earth—just the way Fred liked it. Nothing to make it so that he was someone to remember. And having a bunch of windows reflecting the sun to the road would make someone come and see what the hell it was.

Following Sarah home—he'd learned her name when he heard one of the cashiers say goodbye to her—Fred was careful not to get caught in any of the cameras on the road. He wondered if the bozos that put them up knew how easy they were to avoid. Just sit back far enough that your face is never seen, and wear gloves, especially when you have marks on your hands that can be traced if the camera picks them up.

She pulled into her parking spot and he drove on by her

90

home. Soon, he told himself, soon he'd have all he needed to get into her home, get what he wanted, and show her, by beating her until she bled, what it was like to have someone following them.

Laughing slightly, he pulled out the little book that he'd purchased some time ago. It had puzzles in it that Fred used as a timer. When he finished three of them, then it was time to move. It was getting harder to just do three anymore. He'd become just too smart for them to trip him up anymore.

Finishing up his puzzles, he got out of his car and made his way up to her apartment. Fred was giddy with excitement. And as he stood outside the door for several moments, he had to calm himself twice before he picked the lock. Easy as pie, he told himself — easy as pie.

Opening the door, he found the little woman on the floor, her face turned away from him. Christ, it was like taking shit from a baby. Not even a whimper in his direction. Picking up the salad that was on the table, he put it into the large trash bag that he always brought for things like this. Putting it next to the door with his other tools of his trade, he pulled his mask up over his face and reached down with his gloved hands to pick her up.

Taking her to the bathroom where he would undress her, he made sure that nothing of his body, which was covered with a lab suit from work, touched anything. Fred put all her things in the hamper, where she would have put them, and took her to the bedroom. There, he would have his fun.

Tying her to the bed wasn't without difficulty. Not that it slowed him down, but she only had a bed frame without a head board. Once he got her in the position he wanted her, Fred looked down at her nudity.

"My oh my, those little salads have done you a world of good, haven't they?" He went to the front room and picked up his tools. Pausing in the kitchen, he looked around. He could have sworn that he saw something out of place. Shaking his head, Fred went to the bedroom again. "Let me see. First we're going to start with those pretty little legs of yours. Then we're going to work our way up to that tight belly."

He touched one of her legs, and wondered for a moment if he could take his gloves off and touch her porcelain skin. But he told himself that mistakes like that one would get him killed or caught.

Laying out his tools was like a ritual for him. They laid in the same order, the handles of them in the same direction. There was an extra set of gloves for him, to wipe his face off when he was too hot. He was ready.

Pulling the cat-o-nine tails up to his body, he felt his long dead cock stir. It would never harden. He would never be able to have sex with the thing. And his libido was as dead as his cock. Nothing excited him but this—hurting and then robbing someone who was too stupid to be aware of their surroundings like they should be.

"Mr. Simmons, you're under arrest." He was so startled by the hard voice behind him that he shifted around, his feet getting caught up in the tails of the whip. "You have the right to—"

"What the fuck are you doing here? This isn't your house. Get out of here." He realized that he was sounding like a fool and closed his mouth. The woman arresting him tore off his mask and head gear and put him to his knees.

There was so much he wanted to say right now, but he looked at his fun. It wasn't who he had thought it was. It was his Emmi getting untied and being handed a robe. While his mind was working out how he'd been mistaken, she waved a little wave at him and blew him a kiss. He dodged it like she might touch him, and the police had another little laugh at his expense.

He was read the rest of his rights and put in the back of a van. While being chained to the seat and floor, Fred knew that he was as good as released. They had nothing on him. He'd done nothing wrong. Being in the room with a naked woman? Nothing. He had been invited. The tools that he'd brought? She liked her sex rough. Fred wasn't sure how to get around it being the wrong woman, but he'd get it figured out. He knew, as surely as he was on his way to the police station, that he hadn't been caught, just delayed for a time. Fred Simmons would not spend any time in jail.

# Chapter 7

Rachel was sick to death of having nothing—less than nothing, really. No food, no fun, and certainly no money. Nothing was going her way. She just wanted some money in her pocket, or a single credit card that she could use for the necessities. She really needed some soap and shampoo. Things that smelled pretty, not like Ralph.

And she was beginning to understand why the man had been married four different times. He was not only a pig, but a hog too. He took most of the covers, and ate the biggest portions of anything that they had. It was mostly stolen by her, so she should have gotten the larger share, in her opinion. But she didn't ask anymore. When she had asked just a few days ago, he'd taken her food too, and eaten it. The man was impossible.

And then there was sex with him. When they'd been having sex at her home, she'd make him take a shower first. They took one together, usually, and that started the foreplay, which she'd discovered right away he didn't do well either. So when they were in the bed, he smelled so fresh that she didn't mind going down on him. But here, with the water being something that decided on its own if you had any or not, he'd given up on the simple civility of just washing his hands.

"What have I gotten myself into?"

It was becoming apparent to her that she'd not had it so bad living and being married to Brody. At least he wasn't up in her face about food not being around. Nor did she have to remind him to clean up after himself. He'd reminded her most of the time.

Her mom and dad were at the shelter. The morning of their last day at the hotel the police had come by and "helped" them out of the room. Their small bits of clothing were checked for towels and other things. Mom told her that the only thing they'd been able to take were the half-used bottles of shampoo and soaps. The coffee stuff, like filters, was taken from them as they made their way out the door. She said that she'd felt like a criminal, but was grateful for the few days in the hotel to have a place to sleep.

Brody was really making it hard for Rachel to get what she needed from him. Pacing the small room, she looked around. It was nasty. She'd had no idea that Ralph only cleaned up to come to her house, and she figured that he only had a decent meal when she had the cooks feed him or she took him out. The man was a slob, and he didn't seem to care.

Rachel had wanted to leave him two days ago, when she'd simply asked him to clean up the bathroom when he was done and he slapped her. There was no tone in her voice — she had tried her best to not only keep her voice at a level, low tone, but not curse at him either. And when she hit her head on the counter, the hit had been so fast and brutal, he stood over her and told her that if he wanted to shit on the walls, then it was his home to do so.

She had not just stayed out of his way, but she'd stopped

talking to him altogether. No one hit her, she thought, and got away with it. Rachel would get back at him for it, she had to just time things right. Whenever that time would come was anyone's guess, but she'd get him back.

The police had been searching for her, Dad said. They'd come by the shelter where they were at least once a day. And there didn't seem to be a pattern to their arriving at the place, so Rachel couldn't just slip in and have herself a nice warm shower and a bed to sleep in that didn't have Ralph in it. Nor would the hot meal go unnoticed.

"How far I have failed when I had it all in my hand?" No, she told herself. She hadn't failed at anything. She was simply between things. Getting to Brody was the thing that would get her on easy street — as soon as she found out where Jordan went to school, how he got there, and what time he got off. You know, she told herself with a sad smile, just little things.

Jordan had been, and still was, her ticket. She had only decided to keep him at the last minute, when she realized that things were falling apart. It was to the point of her being without anything if Brody got a burr up his ass, which he had. Then he had to go and lock her out of the house, take her son, and do a test on him that would make sure that he wasn't the father. With or without the boy, she doubted that she'd get anything from him. He might even make her pay him, it was that bad. Rachel just hoped that he never found out about the other brats she'd gotten rid of. That would be, as they say, the nail in her own coffin.

Brody had really fucked up her life getting himself a set of balls. She'd been by the house twice now; once to tear the For Sale sign out of the yard, the second time a few days later to notice that the sign was back and it had a sold sticker on it. Of all the nerve. Again, she wondered if he'd found all her stash. More than likely. It wasn't as if she'd hidden it all that well. Brody never entered their bedroom, so she thought that she didn't need to bother. Fuck.

Brody must have gotten a great deal of money for that sucker too. It was a beautiful home. The walls were all nice and cleaned. She would know that, she supposed, since she hadn't been able to hang so much as a picture on the walls. Of course, she did have a man in their bed not three days after moving into the mansion. But she'd never forgive Brody for laughing at her on their wedding night.

Rachel had spent three months going to the gym to tone up her body. Ate nothing but green food for the same three months. Not a drop of wine either. She'd not had any idea of the number of calories in just one glass of it. She'd not only gotten herself down three dress sizes, but she could swear you could bounce a fucking nickel off her abs. Even her breasts had toned up. Her ass looked fine, and she was really proud of her thighs and calves. Then he'd laughed when she came out in the skimpiest things she could find.

It wasn't until she went back into the bathroom after slapping the piss out of him that she noticed the long trail of toilet paper stuck to her foot. No wonder he'd laughed. Christ, she might have too if it hadn't been their fucking wedding night. And staying in the bathroom all night had gotten her nothing but a kink in her back and a stiff neck.

Brody really had tried hard to make up for it, she remembered now. She really didn't care one way or the other, not then or now. She'd only married him for one thing and one thing only—to get at his money. To control it. To spend it and to be able to tell everyone she knew that she was a doctor's wife.

But it had done her little good. There wasn't anything for her to control, because he did the controlling. She wasn't able to spend money like she was rich and as fabulous as she always thought of herself as being. Not only did all her friends — which she'd had few of that she was close to — stop coming around, but Brody and his giant cock wouldn't sleep with her.

She supposed, now that she thought of it, that it had been stupid to fuck someone else in their house. His house, she meant. He'd not only caught her at it, but he'd not made a big deal out of it either — except, of course, to cut her off more than he already had. There wasn't an account for her to use. All the stores had been told not to give her any kind of credit. The cards had suddenly dried up, and she wasn't able to just pick up the tab for her own luncheon, much less the entire table of women whose group Rachel had shoved her way into.

Getting out of the house, she was careful where she went. The police would pick her up for any number of things that she'd done lately just to get back at Brody. The hospital was the worst, she guessed. They wanted her to not only pay for what it took to get everything repaired the night she'd been there, but to also pay for several pieces of equipment that she supposedly broke on her rampage.

In two days she had to appear before a judge to be told about the divorce and what she wasn't going to get out of it. The list of things that she wasn't getting was longer than the list of things that she wanted or was getting. Her parents had suffered too, her mom told her, when she'd been summoned, but Rachel didn't care about them. They were old and would be dead soon, and she had a lot of life left in her. Life that wasn't going to get her anywhere if she didn't get some money soon.

There was a big to do involving the police at the apartment building that she had wanted to move into when the courts took her home from her. The one that Ralph and she had planned on getting wasn't as big as the one that Brody had, not even close, but it was going to be theirs. Really, when she thought of it now, she was sort of glad that she didn't have a home with Ralph. It was bad enough in the three-room place that he had that he'd trashed. She could only imagine what he'd do to an entire house. That was another thing they were going to tell her, no doubt—that Brody's money had been used to secure the house, so she was shit out of luck. They'd probably be that rude about it too.

Keeping an eye on the police, careful of where they were looking, Rachel watched them take a man out in cuffs. He had a sack or something over his head, but she didn't care who he was. She was just curious about anything going on to break the boredom of Ralph and his dirty habits.

Then a woman came out. As she stood there just behind a gorgeous man, Rachel tried to remember where she'd seen her before. Her body was willow thin, her face like that of an Irish china doll. Her pale skin and long dark red hair just added to her beauty. The color didn't come from a bottle either—that was as natural as everything else about her. She looked like she could take on the world and come out the winner, especially with the man behind her.

When she turned her face to the side to talk to the police, it hit Rachel hard. The woman from the mall—and her son had been with her. What they were doing there was still hard for her to latch onto. She couldn't even remember what she'd been doing there. But the woman—she'd stood up from someplace, and Rachel had felt the need to move on. That—

"She told me that it wasn't Jordan. I asked her for him, demanded that she turn him over to me, and she was—"

Rachel felt the blood come from her nose as she tried harder to reach the information that she needed. She couldn't remember more, but Rachel did know one thing. The woman had her son, and she needed to get him to come home with her. At least until Brody decided to play ball with her on her terms.

Walking back to the house of mess, she wasn't paying any attention to things going on around her anymore. Rachel had a feeling that a great deal was riding on this woman. She was having an affair with Brody. No, that didn't explain the man with her. Brother? Doubtful. He was too close to her for that. Something. He was her protector. For Brody.

Stopping suddenly, she felt someone ram into her from behind. Before she could turn and tell the fucker off, her rights were being read to her and she was down on her knees. Crying because this wasn't helping her plans, she begged the man to let her go. But all she got was a "shut the fuck up and listen" before she was not just put into a cruiser that she'd not noticed, but they'd knocked her head twice before she was shoved into it.

Rachel had no attorney, and no money to pay one. There wasn't anyone that she could call to come and help her out. No one that she even knew slightly would come to her aid. And her parents, they seemed to be happy living at the shelter for now. And soon, because of their age and Dad being a fucking drunk, they'd be out on their ass from there too. She did wonder for a moment where he was getting the cash for that, but the cruiser stopped and she was at the jail. Christ, nothing was fucking going to ever come out the way she wanted it to.

The man in the cell two down from hers was sitting on the floor meditating. He looked like a pretzel sitting there, with his fingers in a circle like he was a stone god or something. Ignoring him, she sat down on the cot. At least the sheets were clean was her first thought.

Lying down, she thought of her life so far. It was shit, she realized. It seemed to her that from the moment she had her fifth birthday — she could remember that she'd gotten nothing that she'd wanted—it had been going downhill. Even fucking her way through high school had gotten her nothing. Her grades were only mediocre, because giving her an A would have been out of the question. Rachel hadn't wanted to go to college, which was good—there wouldn't have been any money for it.

When she'd met Brody and figured out what he did for a living, she thought finally her life was going to turn around. But even that had gone south with the fall. He wasn't any fun, and acted like having money was something that you didn't celebrate with—just invest it to make more of it.

Now, here she sat in jail with nothing. Smiling, she did think that she'd not do a thing differently. While she didn't have anything, Rachel sure had made it an entertaining slide from poor to poorer.

~*~

"The money for the Mabel Little Scholarship is set up just the way you wanted it. And I hope you don't mind, but I have hired an investor to make sure that the funding doesn't deplete much over the years." Brody nodded. He was distracted. "The cash that was found in the house when it was packed up is now set up too. I swear to you, I wish I had thought of setting up a fund with Rachel's name on it. That is going to make her shit a brick when she finds out that there is money out there for people wanting to buy a house and needing help with the funding. You are devious. You know that, don't you?"

Brody looked at Forrest. They'd been working for the last few hours, and he was no closer to figuring out what he should do then he had been this morning when he'd gone out on a call with the police. Forrest asked him to tell him what was going on.

"I'm a good doctor, I think. At least I hope so." Forrest

nodded — non-committal, just what he needed from him. This way he could bounce things off him and not worry about him talking him into something. "This morning I was called to a crime scene. The police don't have a police physician on staff right now and I really am excited about doing — I'm off subject. Not only was I able to tell them things that they might not have seen, but I think I enjoyed it more than I should have."

"Why is that?" He told him. "Just because someone was killed and you helped out does not make you a monster because you had fun, Brody. It means that you're a good person who helped solve their murder."

"I know. But when I got to my car, I was shaking about how much fun it had been. No, not fun — excitement. And that made me feel guilty." Forrest asked him what he'd been guilty of. "That's just it, I'm not sure. Was I giddy — and I mean, I was giddy — because they thought enough of me to call on me? There are several doctors in town that have been here longer than me. Was it because I found a couple of clues that I'm sure the coroner would have found? Or, as I said, am I a monster?"

"Have you met the local coroner?" Brody said he'd not. "I think he was here when the building was built. For all I know, they simply found him and built the building right around him. He's as outdated as the equipment he uses. Did you know that he still writes his notes down as he goes? Without removing his gloves first. Can you imagine the germs and cross DNA that he's fucked up? How many cases might have gone the other way if he'd been a little smarter about what he was doing? Brody, the man smokes while he's doing these things."

Brody laughed. But Forrest told him he was serious. "That's not even right. I mean, other than the writing down, what if he dropped an ash or two in the body? Christ, no wonder they want him to retire soon." Forrest didn't say anything; again, just what he needed. "The thing is, how can I be a doctor, where I help people, if I stick with the job that they offered me today?" He asked if the pay was good. "Yes, I guess. That's not the reason that I was considering it."

"All right. And that was the right answer, by the way. Why did you become a doctor, Brody? I don't mean the motto that hangs in every office from here to Timbuctoo. I mean, why did Brody Downs become a doctor?"

He thought about it for a moment then looked at Forrest. "I wanted to help people to feel like they could make it another day. To reduce the pain where I could—and you'd not believe how often that is simply all they need. And to be there for them when they've taken their last breath or their first. Bringing a child into the world is amazing. But just as amazing in an entirely different way is being there, holding the hand of someone that is just wanting to go to a place to rest." Forrest said that was beautiful. "Thanks. I've been thinking about that too."

"So, you want to help people. Did you help the deceased this morning?" Brody asked him what he meant. "The person that was murdered, you said you found a clue? Do you think that helped that person? Even a little?"

He didn't know what he meant for a moment until bam, it was like he'd hit him in the head. "I did help them—or their families in this case. I might not have eased their suffering when they were being murdered, but I might have been able to give their family some peace. Because when the police are able to use the clue to find the killer, the family will know he or she isn't still out there."

"Right. Now, would you have felt any better if the same victim was to come to your ER and had died there? Do you think you might have been able to find the same clues?" Brody didn't even have to think about it—no, he would not have. "Then all you have to do now is think which one you'd like to do. Because from where I stand. I'd rather have you out in the field than in a room where you can't do anything for me."

Thanking Forrest, he started to leave. Brody had no idea where he was going, but when Forrest called him back, he realized that they still had things to finish up. Sitting down, he felt better than he had this morning, and much better than he had even a week ago. He and Aaron were having an amazing time just simply being together.

"I have something that I'd like for you to read. I don't think that it'll burst your bubble of good mood, but I think you'll love this." He handed him the thick notebook. "That's the book that your father told you about. And he's come to see me a couple of times. He is having a grand time with Jordan too; did you know that?"

"Yes. Dad came to talk to me before he talked to Jordan. He didn't want to freak him out, so we went to talk to him the first time together. Jordan didn't know him. I'd forgotten about that. He died just a few months before I got married." He asked him how that had gone with his dad and Jordan the first time. "Jordan was so overwhelmed to have a real grandda and not one he had to borrow. Dad is even helping him with his homework and the décor in his room. Last night I told Jordan to go up to bed, and Dad asked to sit with him for a while. I guess Dad reads to him. I'm not sure how that works, but that's what he does nightly."

"That's wonderful. And your mom, how is she taking having her husband around again?" Brody laughed when he thought of them together. "I take it he's all right when her being with Howie."

"Oh, yes. Howie was always a good friend more than he

was a butler. But he hung around after I left, and my parents sort of moved him from butler status to being welcome to the table." Brody laughed again. "Mom and Dad fuss at each other just as they did when he was alive. And as for Howie, he's so happy that Mom didn't just sit around pining after Dad when he passed away."

Brody worked with Forrest on his personal things because Jake was working on his divorce. Forrest was also going to be representing Emmi and a lot of other women in the case against Fred Simmons. Brody had gone to see the man—he'd complained about a contusion that the police had given him. While he'd not found anything wrong with the man, he had formed an opinion. The man was cocky.

In addition to the scholarship for Ms. Little and the aid for new homes, there was the paperwork that Brody filled out that gave Aaron authority to make medical and legal decisions about Jordan when necessary. Brody also put Aaron on his insurance plan, made him the second beneficiary to his life insurance, as well as changed the will to include him and exclude Rachel and her parents. They'd be divorced in the morning, he hoped, and he wasn't going to take any chances with his new family.

Forrest asked him about Fred when they were finishing up. Brody asked him what he was allowed to tell him. He'd been acting on the part of the police, not the man, so Forrest said that he could tell him what he wanted.

"Have you ever met a person that you instantly didn't like? They might not have spoken to you, or done a thing to you either. But there is something profound about them that you just don't like." Forrest said that he had. "That's this guy to me. Not only is he cocky, but he's arrogant as well. Like he knows a great deal more than anyone around him. And I also got the feeling, when the police were talking to him as

I worked, that he doesn't believe they have a thing on him. That he's going to walk out of the courthouse a free man to do what he wishes. I do believe that if he does, there won't be any stopping him in hurting the women."

"I've had twenty-three women come forward about having the same thing happen to them. One of them even said that she was sure that there was one more that he'd murdered." Brody asked how she'd come to that. "She said that her friend that she worked with was having the same issue. Black outs. Her body being hurt. I guess at the beginning, he wasn't so violent. Then this friend of hers just disappeared one night. No trace of her, her car was gone, and no one ever heard from her again."

"This is just me thinking outside the box, but why don't you have Cam go and see what he can find out? I've seen him work. The man is amazingly gifted." Forrest told him not to say that to Cam. "Yes, I did, as a matter of fact. I got a ten-minute lecture on how it's ruined his life for the most part. He's very intense, isn't he? But not when he and Rick are together."

"That's the way it should work with mates. Yes, I think you're right. I will have Cam have a look at his head. Can't hurt to get his feelings on this case. And if you're right, and I have no doubt that you are — he is thinking we have nothing — that means we'll have to work harder to find him guilty of all charges. But this woman, I'm looking into her death as well."

Brody was to go to the bank to pick up a credit card with Aaron's name on it, as he'd done the same for him. Aaron had money too, so they'd decided that they'd be a one household bank account, and that had worked out well for them. Brody had never felt that comfortable with Rachel having credit cards, but this man made him feel like he could trust him with it all. But mostly having his son around him.

107

Stopping by the deli to pick up two loaves of bread, he looked over the salad menu and decided to have some lunch. Brody had never been bothered by eating alone. Since he'd been single, even married, it had felt like that. Brody enjoyed the quiet of the hour he allotted himself. Now, he realized he missed the noises that Jordan made while eating. And Aaron filling him in on things that he was working on too.

"You with anyone?" The man sat across from him and Brody looked around. "You must be the good doctor here in town. I was wondering if you had a moment to go over some things that are coming up on the market that I can get you for—"

"No." Brody looked at the shocked look on the man's face. "I want you to pick up your things, get out of the chair, and leave me alone. When and if I need the newest piece of equipment, I will find it myself, after doing a very thorough research of it. Now, I'm having lunch alone for a reason."

He'd never done anything like that before. Usually when a salesperson would bother him, he'd just let them prattle on. But he felt empowered—by love, he realized. When the man hesitated just a little too long, Brody pointed at the police who were having lunch in the restaurant too. And the man, whoever he was, got up and moved on. Brody wanted to celebrate. He'd been no ruder than the man had been by sitting down. But when the second man sat down, Brody sat up straighter in his seat.

# Chapter 8

Willy Henderson liked this young man. He reminded him of Cam a great deal. And after talking to his grandson about him, he'd decided to go and see him for a few things. He looked like a man with a head on his shoulders who knew just how to use it.

"Mr. Henderson, what can I do for you? And I wanted to thank you for taking Jordan under your wing. He's been thrilled to death to have you in his life, and Mrs. Jamison."

"Okay, first, I'm Willy. That two-faced bastard of a son of mine is Mr. Henderson. You heard about him?" Brody nodded and said that he was sorry. "No need for you to be sorry, young man. He was a pole cat that has finally gotten his just desserts. Damned boy. You'd think with me and his mom there, he might have turned out a bit better. I guess there is no accounting for good genes. And that boy of yours, he's a good one. You know, it took damned near a week for him to stop calling me Mr. whatever. You gonna give me trouble?"

"No, sir. I don't think I will." They both laughed. "Did you want something to eat? I just sat down, and since it's only a salad, I don't mind waiting on you to talk to you."

Willy got up and got him some lunch. He wasn't a big man, tall but not fat. But he ate like he was never going to get another meal most times. Today wasn't any different. When he was brought his food on a tray, he handed Brody some of the cookies he'd gotten, as well as a sandwich. He'd gotten them both a more hearty meal.

Neither said much as they ate the food, then when Brody pushed his plate away, he leaned back in the chair. Willy watched him look him over, and hoped that he'd not find him lacking. He didn't have any idea why, but he wanted to be someone this kid could be friends with.

"Now, how about you tell me why you fed me enough to fatten me up, and I'll tell you the answer the best way I know how. However, Willy, you should know that I don't pull punches with family." Willy smiled at him. Just what he wanted to hear. "Also, I'd really enjoy it if you and Ann would join us for dinner tonight. Aaron is still out of town."

"He's a good man too, you know." Brody nodded. "Anyway. I was just over at Forrest's offices, and I heard about your setting up some kind of scholarship programs or something."

"Yes. A woman that I knew in my practice—she was a cantankerous thing—told me that she had no one left to be with. I'd been caring for her for ten years or so, and when I told her that I was getting a divorce, I'll not say what she called my wife, but she said that would make her happy. She died that afternoon, leaving me everything." Willy asked how much it was. "Just under nine million. And as I've done well with my own money and have invested well, I didn't really need it. So, I thought it would be of better use to those that needed it much more than I did."

"Now, that's what I'm talking about. See there—if my son had done something like that, even one time, I might have

110

had a better opinion of him." Willy thought about it. "Nah, he was an asshole, and I didn't care for the way he treated my grandchildren. I would like to help out with that."

"You mean distribute it?" Willy explained. "Oh, add to it. Sure, that would be great. At this point Forrest is putting it together to make it work. But sure, that would be wonderful. I was calling it the Mabel Little Scholarship, but if you'd prefer something different, then we can work with that too."

"No, that's a perfect name for it. She was elderly then?" Brody told him that she was one hundred and four. "I'm an immortal. I'm still trying to come to terms with that. But if I can be around family all the time, you all, then I think it'll make it easier on my old mind. You—you and your family— you're gonna be around for a while too, I'm assuming."

"I didn't know about it until my guy at the gate told me that I was like him. Immortal. I have been meaning to ask someone about it, but with my soon to be ex wandering around, I've been distracted." Willy told him what he knew. "Never ill either, huh? That's great. But I don't want to never grow old while my son does. For that matter, I don't want him to stay a child either, I guess."

"That's not how that part works. You see, Jordan, he'll not die either. But as he grows older and hits a certain age—I think they told me about twenty-five—he'll remain that age. I guess you being older now, you'll be what you are now. No going backwards." Willy laughed as he continued. "Sure would be nice some days if I could. Just to roll back time so that I can do the things a younger man does."

"I'm sure that once you set your mind to something, Willy, you do it." They both laughed, and one of the staff came over and took away their used plates. "Willy, we've been all over the place here, money to age. Why don't you tell me why you're really here?"

"Smart man. I knew you were." He looked around, then leaned in to speak quietly to Brody. "I'm a man in his nineties. I have a good ticker, and I'm not going to keel over if I have sex at my age. Always scared me, I have to tell you. I'd like to know if you can help me out with something to help me...you know...I need help in the sex department."

It only took the man a second or two until he understood. Brody didn't smile at him, never snickered, nor did he ask him if he was sure. All he did was ask him if he knew the side effects. Or did he want to come into his office for some samples to see if it helped him before having to buy them.

Willy wanted to cry. A grown man, and he could feel his eyes just about to spill out some fat tears. And that kid across from him never said nary a word, never made fun of him or even teased him about the situation, nor that he was crying about how relieved he was. As he sat there, holding onto himself, Brody told him that some people his age didn't like the side effects, and he'd very much like to take his blood pressure just once to be sure.

"Yes, I can do that." Brody didn't say anything more as Willy continued to look out the window. "I'd like for you to do something else for me, young man. If you don't mind. I know you don't have anyone left in the grandparent department, and if you don't mind, I'd truly like it if you got around to calling me Grandda. It sure would make my heart just about sing with happiness if you'd do that."

"It would be my honor, Grandda."

Willy got up. But before he left the table, he noticed that Brody had put a twenty under the tea glass that had been his. No need to tip here, but he'd done it all the same. Willy had to leave now or he was going to be begging the man to let him adopt him.

On his way to Brody's office, he thought about the

scholarships that had been set up by him. There wasn't any reason for him to do it, Willy thought, other than he could. That's what he'd like to do. Get something set up so that kids, or even adults, could go to college, or even just to get their high school education.

That's it, he nearly screamed. He was going to talk to Forrest or Jake about setting up a program to help out older adults to get their education. Or even to take a few classes that they'd like to see if they enjoyed. He had done it three or four times in his later years — gone to college to look into things. He knew how to throw a pot now, develop film, and even to fix a television should he have a desire to. Yes, that was it, he was going to make a difference.

Pulling into the office, he noticed that there wasn't much in the way of parking in the area. Hell, he thought, there was little to nothing other than his office in this area. There was a defunct pizza place, and another shop that had been a candy shop. Also, and this one saddened him a great deal, the florist was gone. He remembered when he was here before his wife had passed away, getting her flowers.

Brody was there a few minutes later. They talked about the area, and he told him about the job that he'd been offered. It sounded to Willy like it was a done deal in him taking it, but Brody was very cautious to keep saying he'd not decided yet. The boy was as good as hired, Willy thought.

"Now, let's see what we have here." It only took a few seconds for Brody to gather up what he needed. Brody put the meds, as he called them, in a plain white bag so that no one would notice. And as he was standing there, squeezing the life out of his arm, Willy noticed that Brody was happy. It nearly blinded a man if he knew what to look for.

There were no more lines around his eyes. His mouth wasn't tensed up like it had been. Ann had remarked to him just the other day how she felt sorry for Brody, what with this divorce going on. He asked Brody, when he was done, when the court date was. He didn't answer him until after he'd listened to his heart and checked his eyes and ears.

"In the morning." He told him that his pressure was great and that he was more confident of him enjoying life. "Also, your heart sounds good. You have no cataracts and nothing that I can see from here that would cause you any trouble with what we discussed. But, just for safety's sake, I'd only take about half a dose and work up to it. I put you a pill cutter in there as well."

"Should I come see you after I take one?" Brody told him only if he thought it was necessary, but that he could stop by anytime. "I don't have any trouble having sex, you see. It's the staying power that I'm sort of lacking in."

Willy felt better talking about this thing in the office. Brody was a doctor and this was his office. Somehow he felt less embarrassed. Brody seemed to understand and sat down on the stool across from him.

"Grandda, the fact that you're having sex at all is astounding to me." They both laughed, and Willy knew he'd be all right. "As I said, watch out for the side effects, and make sure you follow the directions correctly. If Ann were to touch them, there could be reactions for her too. And not in a good way. Since we're both immortal, I don't have a problem with you having some fun, but just do it in moderation."

"You knew it was Ann." Brody said that he was sorry if he was wrong. "You're not. Ann and I have been together for some time now. And I teased my son about banging her — not a nice term, but he pissed me off — and then having us a kid. I know we neither one can, but you know how kids can be."

"I do. I sometimes think that Jordan does it to see how far he can push me. Which is fine. Boundaries for kids are how they learn rules. Jordan is a good kid, but there are times when he's not." Willy said he knew that for sure. "Cam is going to do something for me today. I'm slightly worried what he'll find once he does his little dance thing through Rachel's head. I'm worried what sort of monstrosity he'll find once he's there."

"I hear that he is going to look though that other man's head too. The guy who hurt our Emmi. If I had gotten to him first, they'd sure be looking for the next terrible man. I don't cotton to hurting women, especially if they're smaller and got babies. There might be some out there that need it, but so far, I've not encountered any." Brody said that they were out there. And were just as bad if not worse than men. "Sad state of affairs that people can't just be kind to each other. Work things out with words and not fists."

After leaving the office with the meds and a good bill of health, he made his way to his home he was sharing with Ann. It was just a rental, but he decided that he wanted to be here for a while. The two of them had been traveling for a long time, not putting any roots down. Willy wanted to stick around and see kids being born, or in some cases, being brought into the family.

He knew that the men were all homosexuals. And thirty years ago, or even less, he might have had a problem with them living like they were. But times had changed, and so had his opinion about them. First, he thought that it wasn't any of his business what others did behind their own doors. And secondly, he wasn't anyone to pass judgement on anyone else. What they did, they did, so long as no harm came to him or those that he loved. And Willy loved every damned one of them. He was going to talk to Ann as soon as she got back from her meeting. Maybe, Willy thought, he'd fix it up so he'd have a few meetings of his own that he needed to go to.

Work, that's what he needed. And involvement. If he had those, he'd not be looking for trouble all the time. And he had been—just waiting for something he could get into and not care what the consequences were.

Thinking about things, he was making a list when his Ann came home.

"Ann dear, I have me something I think you're going to enjoy. I know I sure will." He picked her up and swung her around. "I want you to marry me, if you have a mind, and us buy us a house. Whatcha say?"

Her giggling was the best thing he'd heard. Yes, Willy was going to get to work living.

~*~

The courtroom was filled to bursting. Brody was glad that they'd arrived early for this, or they might have been standing in the hall when they needed him. Maybe, he thought, that's where I'd like to be. Not that he was worried about the outcome. They had enough shit on Rachel that he was sure that some of it she might even have forgotten. The only thing that wasn't on her list of crimes was bank robbery. And he wouldn't put it past her to try sometime soon.

Jordan had been asked to come to the courthouse today too. Brody wasn't so sure about that, having him there to hear all the things about his mom. But Jake had told him that they'd try and make it easier for him. He didn't know how that was going to come about—his ex-wife was worse than even he'd thought.

After they were settled again after the judge came in, both Jake and the court appointed attorney stood. Then they brought in Rachel. My God, Brody thought, how the bitch has fallen. Even Jordan whistled quietly.

"Thank you for coming, everyone." The judge, Judge Samuel Bask, looked at Jordan. "Young man, I do want to thank you for coming in as well. And as best we can, we'll try to keep this clean and non-violent. You and I will talk after this is done."

"Yes, sir." Judge Bask winked at Jordan. "Sir, can I ask you just one thing? I promise you that it's important, and I'll take you at your word. But I'd like to come up there, if you don't mind."

No one told him no, and the judge waved him to come up to the front. The attorneys for both sides followed, and Jordan leaned in to whisper in Bask's ear. It didn't take him long, but whatever he'd said had shocked the older man. Judge Bask then told both Brody's attorney and Rachel's what was said. Whatever it was had Jake winking at Jordan.

"Doctor Downs. Did you know that I was going to have this short conversation with your son?" Rachel yelled that it was her son. "You just pipe down there, young lady. Believe it or not, I'm in charge here today. Well, Doctor Downs?"

"No sir. And if it offended you in anyway, I'm truly sorry. While I don't know what he said, I'm sure that he'd thought about it a great deal before talking to you." Judge Bask looked at Jordan again as Brody continued. "He's a good son, sir. And I can't tell you that he'll not do it again. To me, it's good to lay all your cards out. And I'm beginning to think that Jordan being taught the same thing has stuck, don't you?"

"Good for you. And no, I didn't find it offending. The truth never is. The fact is, he is terrified of his mother and her boyfriend, which I find putting the cart before the horse. But then, I'm old fashioned like that. But he in no way wants to be with her. He said he'd rather go to military school than to have to live with her."

Brody just looked at Jordan and then hugged him. Rachel was screaming that he was her son, but nothing more was said about it. For as long as he lived, Brody would never

KATHI S. BARTON

forget these words, and how much he dearly loved Jorden.

The courtroom was put back to order and they began. The first person that Jake called was Rachel. It was his plan to get the shit out of the way so that she'd not be able to say what a good mom she had been.

"Ms. Downs, I would like for you to read over this paperwork before we proceed." She took it but didn't look at it. "You don't want to look over the prenup that you signed with Dr. Downs?"

"No, I know what it says. It says that I get nothing. But I have a son that he took from me, and I want to raise him myself. With money provided to me by him." She pointed at him and Brody watched her. "I put up with him for ten years. Getting up and leaving me in the middle of the night. Having to leave birthday parties for my son."

"I'm glad that you brought that up. Because I have pictures here of all of Jordan's birthday parties, and there is no picture of you. Plenty with Brody and Jordan. Even a couple of times with his grandparents. Christmas is like that as well. There are no pictures of you at any time with your son during any—"

"Who do you think took the pictures, you moron?" She was told to behave. "Seriously, is that all you have? If so, I'd like to get down to the fact that I have nothing. My home has been taken from me. Even the one that I was trying to set up to leave Brody. He was an abusive man. I tell you, he hit me daily."

"Dr. Downs hit you?" Jordan jumped up and screamed at his mom that she was lying. "I don't think we could get a better witness than your son about that, do you?"

But Jordan wasn't finished. "She was never there for anything but having men over to the house. And all my parties were fun because she wasn't there. She was mean to

118

me, and Mr. Ralph was mean to me too. I don't want her to take me nowhere. Ever." Jordan looked at Brody, tears in his eyes. "Please, Dad, please don't let her take me from you. I want to live with you and Grandma. If you make me go with her, I'll run away and you'll never find me again."

Brody held his son while Judge Bask called a recess. And then he asked to see Jordan. When his son was about to go in the back with the man, he came back and hugged him, telling him how much he loved him. Then he walked by his mother and said not a single word.

Everyone just sat in their seats. While Brody didn't know what was going on back there, he wasn't worried for his son. He'd talked to him before leaving the house this morning, and told him that he'd hear things that weren't nice, but that he had to believe that they had nothing to do with him. This was all about Brody and Jordan's mom.

It was about an hour before Jordan and the judge came out of the back room. Jordan had been crying more, and he worried about him. But when the judge told him that he could go with his grandma now, Jordan kissed Brody on the cheek and left the courtroom with Howie and Brody's mom. Brody turned around and waited for whatever happened next.

"Proceed."

The judge was then handed the notebook that had been at the other surgeon's office. Brody sort of tuned things out while thinking of all the other stuff he had going on right now. The book had some damning information in it, and he just didn't want to hear it again. Reading it was bad enough.

Rachel had had forty-three abortions in her lifetime. Two to three a year, it looked like. There was never a year that passed after she turned fifteen where she'd not had at least one. And there was never a name that went with the dates, other than hers. Rachel never filled in who the potential father might have been. Brody wondered if it was because she couldn't remember or just didn't care. She'd not even bothered to change her name to something else to hide her actions.

She was shameless, Jake had told him. She didn't care what she did or who she did it to, as long as she could get what she wanted. And she had no remorse. If asked, Jake said to him, he'd bet that she'd say that it was better to abort the children than to have to abandon them someplace. It would be just like her, he was beginning to think, to do just that.

When his name was said, he turned and looked around the big room. Rachel was gone, and the guard standing in front of him had his gun out. It took him a few seconds to realize that something had happened and he had zoned out. Jake came to ask him if he was all right.

"Yes. I think so. I was deep in thought." Jake laughed and said no shit. "Where is Rachel? Please tell me that she didn't get away. Jordan is out there."

"No. She's fine, more's the pity. I can't believe that you missed it all. A man—his name was on the list of fathers—came in here to kill her. I didn't catch it all. I was trying my best not to get myself killed. But when he took out a knife and threw it in her general direction, she hit the floor and so did I. And you can't believe what I was thinking when I looked to see if you'd been hurt, and you're just sitting there, like it's an everyday occurrence for you to have a mad man come in and try to slice up everyone. Brody, you need to get out more."

He looked around again, this time looking for things he'd not seen the first time. A knife was still stuck in the place above where Rachel had been sitting. Turning around, he could see the doors open and a medic team working. They'd killed the man with the knife, Jake told him, before he could come in and kill anyone.

Rachel was brought back out, screaming about how this was all his fault. Jake told him not to engage with her, that he'd take care of it. When the judge, who was obviously shaken up, told her to sit down and shut the fuck up, she did so immediately. But she glared at Brody the entire time.

"Ms. Downs, why is it that man was saying that you took his child from him?" Jake moved to sit in front of him, blocking Rachel from being able to see him. Brody was glad for that. She was giving him the evil eye. "Ms. Downs, that man thought that you took his child from him. Was he the real father of Jordan?"

"I don't know." She tried to look around Jake. "Why is it he gets to sit there in a nice suit, and I can't even get anyone to bring me a decent meal?"

"Because, and this might surprise you, he's not done anything wrong." Jake picked up the sheets of paper that had been copied from the notebook. "I was wondering if he could be the father of the child you aborted on January seventeenth of six years ago. Or perhaps the one that you aborted in June of the same year."

"What are you talking about? This has nothing to do with what I did in my personal life. This has to do with Brody throwing me to the wolves and leaving me with nothing. I want my son to come and live with me, and for him to pay child support so that I can raise him like I'm used to having Jordan raised."

"*You're* used to having him raised? I wasn't aware that you had anything to do with the upbringing of young Jordan. Why, if you want him so badly, are you looking into military schools for him? Or for that matter, talking to your mom about her taking him off your hands and you'll pay her for it?" Rachel asked Jake where the fuck he'd gotten that idea. "From you and your computer searches. You did read that

121

they keep track of the sites that you visit while in jail, didn't you? Also, they record every conversation that you have when you have a visitor. Then when they find something that isn't right, such as pawning off your son to someone that doesn't want him without more money, then they let someone know. In this case, me. And you didn't answer the questions about the abortions either. We can go over each of the forty plus of them if that'll help you remember who he might have been."

"Again, you moron, what does that have to do with today? I just want to go home, to my home, and bring my son with me. I want Brody to pay for us to live together in my house I had paid for, and for you cock suckers to leave me alone." Jake handed a sheath of papers to the judge. "What are you doing? This is between us right now."

"Your Honor, as you can see by the list there that was obtained from a retired doctor, Ms. Downs had a number of abortions while married to Dr. Downs." He handed him the signed statement that said that Brody hadn't slept with his wife for many years before she told him that she was pregnant with his child. "On the next page there, Your Honor, you'll see the blood tests done on Jordan Downs on the day he was born. Dr. Downs has known since Jordan was born that he wasn't his son. Yet he continued to raise him like he was. Providing for him when he needed, getting up in the middle of the night with him. Taking him to school and other functions as any biological father would have done. And all the time, he knew that Rachel was having affairs. But he had Jordan, and that was enough. But she began stealing valuable items from the house and selling them to finance not only her forty plus abortions, but also to purchase a house that she was going to have Brody pay for while she lived there with her lover."

"Ms. Downs, were you aware that nothing in the house

belonged to you?" Rachel said that Brody had told her that almost daily. "Then you blatantly stole things from the house to finance this other life that you wanted to have with another man?"

"What was I supposed to do? He gave me one of those prepaid credit cards after we got back from our special honeymoon."

The judge looked at Brody, asking if it was special.

"It was special all right, Your Honor. She had a man in the bed when I returned from getting breakfast the morning after we were wed. And when I asked her about it, she told me that he was just some random man that had come by, and she decided that he'd be more fun than me." The people in the courtroom murmured about that for five minutes. Then Brody continued. "On the way back from Paris, she told me how she'd joined the Mile-High Club. It wasn't with me."

"I told you, he was boring. Not to mention, he laughed at me on our wedding night. How else did you propose I get back at him?"

Brody told the courtroom about the toilet paper and how he'd been unable to stop. No one in the courtroom could stop laughing either, and Judge Bask was doing his best to not join them. In the end, he burst out laughing as well.

"As you can tell, that's just the way I reacted. But after she hit me and stayed in the bathroom all night, I decided to go and get her flowers and give her breakfast in bed. That's what I came back to." He handed Jake the name of the waiter that Rachel had hooked up with in the hotel. "Also, as you can see from the birth certificate that was in her possession, his is one of the names listed on the back. It must have been an ongoing affair with that man."

No one said anything more while the judge looked over the paperwork. Brody took that time to look at Rachel. Christ, how had he ever thought that he was in love with her? Not to mention, why did he stay with her for so long? That was a question that Jake was going to ask him, and he was no closer to figuring it out than he had been before. Shaking his head, the judge asked for everyone to have a seat. Rachel was moved back to her place at the other table.

"I've never seen a couple so unsuited, yet who stayed together for ten years. I'm assuming for the sake of the child, Dr. Downs." Brody stood and said that was it mainly. "Yes, well, you're a good man by all accounts. And my mother just simply loves you to pieces, I might add. And she's not the only one either. When my family found out that you were getting a divorce and trying to keep your son, you'd not believe the hate mail I got."

"I'm sorry, Your Honor, but I do want my son with me. I'll do whatever it takes, within reason." Judge Bask looked at him, then at Rachel. "I'm very sorry that others seem to think I'd not be a good role model to Jordan. I'll try harder, I swear it."

Rachel snorted.

"Yes, I'm sorry. It wasn't hate mail to have you not get Jordan, young man, but that if I didn't rule in your favor." He reached behind him and pulled out a stack of papers, then a second one. "This is the mail that I received only yesterday. The post office is making a killing off this, and there is not one letter or email to me that claims you to be anything but what you are—a good man trying to raise a good boy into a better man. I, for one, thank you for that. And for that, I give Dr. Brody Downs full custody of Jordan Conrad Downs. And as of this day at this time, I formally deem Rachel Sharp Downs and Brody Conrad Downs's marriage dissolved. Court adjourned. Ms. Downs, your hearing will be in one hour. Do not leave this building."

124

# Chapter 9

Jake was waiting for the hour to be up so that he could get to the next part of the trial for Rachel. It was mostly about the damage that had been done to the hospital when she'd gone there to look for Brody, but there were a couple of things that he wanted to bring up as well. Brody had called home to let them know the outcome of the divorce, and Jake, for one, was happy to have that part over with.

He did not envy Forrest in the next trial against Fred Simmons. Cam had gone looking for the man's information, and what he'd gotten was a great deal more than they'd thought they would. But the issue was, for now, that they couldn't move on it—on any of it—because the man was in jail and they didn't want the newspapers and such to get hold of it as yet.

"The Feds are all over the property, but they're hiking in from the back end. His uncle on his mother's side owns it, so that is why it wouldn't have been traced back to him. Brody, there are at least three dozen cars there. All of them so far that we've checked are registered to unsolved missing persons." Jake had asked Cam if there was any way to attach them to

Simmons. "That's what we're looking for. My men are out there now working to find any fingerprints, DNA, anything to show that he had something to do with the cars. If we could find his stash—the things in his head were a little unclear as to where they were hidden—that would go a long way to helping us. I was thinking about sending Quincey to see him to search face to face, but I don't think that'll work. He'll kill the man."

Jake had no doubt that he was right about that. But Emmi said that she wanted to allow the other women, and now the families of the missing, to be able to know about their absent family members. It would be nice, but Jake was only hoping to get him in prison for a while. But Forrest had it worked out, he said, that Simmons would be gone a long time. And Jake was going to second chair it with him.

The next trial for Rachel was just beginning when the attorneys were called to the back room. He didn't know what had happened, but he was worried all the same. As soon as they entered the nicely appointed room, Judge Bask was nowhere to be seen. Jake asked the bailiff what was going on.

"We have a problem. And I think you can help me with it, Jake. Christ, I hope so." He nodded and told the bailiff whatever he needed. "Samuel is down the hall. He's having chest pains."

Without asking, Jake stepped out of the room and called for Brody. He supposed there was some look on his face, because Brody didn't ask any questions but moved to him. Telling him what he knew, Jake ran out to Brody's Jeep to get his bag. He supposed, as a doctor, he didn't go anywhere without it.

Jake kept the crowd of employees out of the way while Brody worked. He talked quietly to the elderly man and examined him at the same time. The ambulance arrived just as Brody was telling him he didn't think it was a heart attack, but there was no point in taking any chances. Then he scolded the man.

"You need to start eating better, Samuel. I told you that the last time I saw you. Your blood pressure is a little high today, higher than I'd like it, and you still need to shed those forty pounds." Brody looked around the room. "Which one of you brought him the cheeseburger and fries with a milk shake chaser for lunch?"

When someone raised their hand, Brody did the same to the man. No one told Brody that he was certainly overstepping his bounds, but they listened when he said what the judge was going to have to start eating daily, as well as following the exercise program that he'd suggested.

"It's no longer suggested to you that you should exercise or eat better, Samuel. You will do it, or the next time I'm kneeling over you, you'll be a dead man that I've just pronounced. Got it?" Samuel said that he did, and they loaded him up on the gurney. "I'm talking to your wife too. I warned you I would if you didn't do it."

"She's going to be none too happy with me. You know that, don't you?" Brody just crossed his arms over his chest. "Yes, all right. I know I have to do it, and from now on, these people here will help me. Won't you?"

Everyone agreed as their boss and good friend was being taken away. His wife showed up just as he was being put in the ambulance, and Brody with him. Whatever was going to happen, Jake would bet anything that it would be done—

The ambulance stopped and Jake was asked to come forward. He stepped up to the opening at the back end of it and asked what he needed. Samuel's secretary came to stand next to him, with the attorney for Rachel on the other side.

"The doc here is telling me that I have to take some time

off. A week at the least." Jake told Samuel that he thought that was a good idea. "I'm glad you agree, young man. I hereby pass my duties on to you as of this moment. Judge Winslow, thank you for your help."

Jake was still standing there when someone tapped him on the shoulder. He wasn't sure what had just happened. Looking at Peter Goff, the secretary to the judge asked him to come inside, there were papers he had to sign.

After putting his name to three of the documents that named him as sitting judge, Jake stopped in the middle of writing his name and looked at Peter. The man was grinning like a loon.

"What's just happened?" He told him. "Oh no. No, I'm not his replacement. I have trials that I have— No, and hell no."

"I'm afraid that you've already signed off on taking the job, Judge Winslow. And I have to tell you, sir. Your grandma, she'd have been tickled pink over this." Jake was still shaking his head when he was fitted for a robe and told what the next three cases were, one of which was his. "I've called Forrest. He's coming in to see to the trial with Rachel. I'm sure that he knows as much about it as you do."

"He does. But I can't be judge. I'm an attorney." Peter told him that was the way it worked out most times. And all the way up until he was sitting at the big boys' dais, he kept saying that he wasn't going to do it.

"Hello, Your Honor." Jake wanted to get up and punch Forrest in the face. "Your Honor, the next case is...."

As Forrest told him about the case, Jake tried to tell himself that he was only helping out. But he had a feeling, a dreadful feeling, that this wasn't going to be temporary. He was going to be stuck here for the rest of his unnatural life.

There wasn't a jury for this against Rachel. She planned to

plead guilty, and they were all hoping that stuck. But almost as soon as he was briefed, on his own case, Rachel was saying how she wasn't going to do anything of the kind, as she was being railroaded. Then she saw him up at the dais.

"What the holy fuck are you doing there?" Jake told her to behave or he'd find her in contempt of court. "I don't give two shits about being held at all. Let me go, and I won't tell everyone in here about you and that man of yours."

Most of the town knew that he and Forrest were lovers. And they all knew that he and Forrest had adopted his little sister. So he just leaned back in his seat and told her to have at it. For some reason, she just stared at him, confused looking.

"You don't care?" Jake told her that the only people that were upset about him being with another man were her and his father. "I know your dad. He was railroaded as well. I want to be set free."

"All right." She asked him if he was serious. "Yes, completely. When you can pay what you owe for the damage you did to the hospital walls and the equipment that had to be replaced. And from what I remember from the briefs, Dr. Downs is suing you for mental anguish over how you've been stalking him."

"It doesn't count as stalking unless you can prove it. I was very careful about how I searched for him. Besides, if he'd just given me what I wanted, then I'd have not had to resort to other means." Jake waited about half a breath before he asked her what those other means might be. "I was going to take my kid. If you remember from this morning, that other judge said that he wasn't Brody's. But I was going to hold him until Brody paid me money that I needed, or he wasn't going to ever find him again. And don't tell me that's kidnapping, because I never found where Brody was hiding him. And he's my son, not his. I don't care what that guy said."

129

"Not any more, he's not yours. Brody has been granted full custody of Jordan. And as of this morning, you are no longer married to him." She just waved him off. "Ms. Sharp, do you have any idea that just telling me about you trying to kidnap your son to hold for ransom is against the law?"

"I don't think I should have to remind you that I didn't actually go through with it. I was only planning it. All he had to do was give me some money. A lot of it. And that would have been easy for him since he has billions of it." Jake looked at Forrest, who was leaning against the table with Rachel's attorney. "He doesn't know what he's talking about, and I decided that I have to know more than some homo does. Isn't that right?"

She was looking at Forrest and the other man—Jake thought his name was Dogwood or something like it. The other man just waved at Rachel, telling her to go ahead, she seemed to be on a roll now.

"See, he agrees with me that I'm smarter than him."

Jake didn't know what to do and reached out to Forrest.

*Let her go. She's hanging herself all by herself. Just keep asking her about things that are crimes like you are. Sheesh, how the hell did he spend ten years with this nutball?* Jake said he had no idea. *By the way, we are so celebrating this promotion tonight. The is a great feather in your hat. Grandma Jenna is right behind you cheering you on.*

It suddenly hit him how much he missed her. Not only did he miss her, but he wanted her to hold Jenna and see that she was crawling now, trying to pull herself up on things. And eating with her fingers. He watched Rachel without hearing her for several minutes until he could gather himself. Then he asked her to repeat herself.

"I said that when Ralph and I get the money back that was in the house before Brody locked me out, then we'll just mosey on down the road and find us a better place. That way Brody can't say shit about us having Jordan. Then he will pay me support. The way I want to be living."

"Rachel, there are laws against everything you're telling me. You can't kidnap a child that isn't yours. You most certainly can't mosey down the road and expect Brody to be happy with you having Jordan. As I have said to you several times now, you are no longer the parent of Jordan. Brody—"

"Brody. Brody. Brody. When does someone say that Rachel has it? The money or the kid? Christ, the way you keep repeating yourself, you'd think you had some rocks loose. I guess that's what being a homo gets you. Nuts." Jake told her that would be enough. "No, I don't think it is. I'm not paying for shit. I'm going to get my son, and I'm going to get money. You aren't going to be able to do anything to me, because I know the rules too, dumbass. You can't have me arrested because I just said that to you."

"I'm not a priest. You can't confess all your misdeeds to me and expect for them to just be ignored." She said that she could because she'd just done it. "Rachel, what is wrong with you?"

She sat down at the other table, then got up and crawled onto the top of it and laid down. No one moved to remove her, but they were all watching her closely. There was something wrong with her, and he'd bet anything that it had been catching up with her all this time and was showing itself today.

"My head hurts really bad." Jake asked Peter to call an ambulance for her. "I don't think that things are right in my head. And my nose is bleeding again."

Jake cautioned everyone to steer clear of Rachel until the ambulance got there. He was worried about a lot of things with her, mostly because he knew that she wasn't the same woman he'd met with a few weeks ago. There was something wrong with her.

As soon as the ambulance arrived, Rachel started throwing up. They were strapping her onto the gurney when she started bolting up from it. Her back was ramrod stiff and her face was contorted, as if in pain. Rachel Sharp Downs was dead before she made it to the hospital.

~*~

Brody was sitting in the living room, all the lights off and the shades drawn. The solitary light in the room was the fireplace that was only on because he'd felt stupid just sitting there without doing anything. He wasn't sure what he was to think or do right now.

His mom sat down next to him and didn't say a word for a long time. "I just got a call from the hospital. Rachel had a tumor in the back of her head." Brody said he knew that. "I'm sorry, son. I don't know what you're feeling, but I do hurt for you. No one seemed to have any idea that she'd been that ill. I mean, we knew she was a little odd, but not like this. Also, Jordan, he's with his Grandda Henderson right now."

"He said that he'd like to just sit with him. I didn't see any harm in it. I know that they're not related in any way, but Jordan has taken a liking to both Willy and Ann." Mom nodded. "It had been there for some time, they said. The tumor. It wasn't until she was under all this stress from what was going on that it started to move and grow. Doctor Fleming, he did the autopsy and called me a bit ago. He told me that there wouldn't have been anything anyone could have done for her even if she'd been on the operating table. The tumor caused a blood clot that broke off and entered her heart. No one could have foreseen it. The only pain she had was the headache. He assured me that the shaking was her body reacting to a foreign object. He said he thought it was trying to take care of it. She didn't feel a thing."

"Did Cam see it? When he was looking for evidence, did he happen to see it there? Or do you know?" Brody had wondered the same thing until he'd heard from Cam. He said that he'd not looked for it because he'd had no idea. Brody told his mom that. "I believe him, do you?"

"Absolutely. He felt horrible about not looking for it. But who would have known to ask him to do that? Like you just said, Mom. She was a little off, but nothing that would have led us to believe that she had a tumor in her brain." Mom told him again how sorry she was. "I don't know how I feel. I'm sorry that she's gone, I truly am. But I'm also relieved that she isn't going to be able to hurt Jordan anymore. I think that he feels the same way, if you want to know the truth. Some of the things that Rachel told Jake, they were scary."

Jake had wondered if the tumor that had been there was responsible for her telling the truth when he met him at the hospital after she had been brought in. He told him how she'd been just babbling about what she was going to do. Quincy said that he'd done that, made her tell everything she had in her head. He'd visited her while she'd been in the jail cell. And no, he'd not seen the tumor either. It seemed that they were all unaware of it, as he'd been.

He looked at Mom. "Ralph contacted me. He wanted to know if I'd have her buried next to his parents. I almost told him that it wasn't for me to decide. He told me how he'd loved her, despite them having fights all the time, and that he'd hit her. I'm not sure how I feel about that either. Then not ten minutes after I got off the phone with him, her parents called. They don't have the funds to bury her. They asked for me to take care of it please, and somehow they'd pay me back. I'm not worried about that. I'm just happy to help them out. They want her buried next to David's parents, where

133

they have plots too." Mom told him that she had heard that as well. "Like I said, I'm going to do it, if for no one else but Jordan. But I'm not going to bury her anywhere but where her parents want her. Ralph is shit out of luck, I feel. They're the ones that need this more than a two-bit thief that had an affair with my wife."

"Brody, I have something to ask you. And you can tell me no or not. But I do think that you should have Jordan go to the funeral. Please?" Brody didn't say anything. He didn't want to go either, but would. "He might not care for her right now. And for all we know, he never will. But he should be there when they put his own mother in the ground. I'll be there with him, and so will you and Howie. Even the dead have said they'd be there for him. But she was his mom, and this is something that he can never go back and fix. Like I said, son, I don't know that he'll ever get over not liking her, but he might need this for some closure."

"I'll talk to him." She thanked him. "Aaron is coming home tomorrow afternoon. He's decided that he's going to give notice for his job. He said that now that he has a family and we can't seem to have a day without something going wrong, he'd rather be here with all of us. I don't want him to quit for that reason, but I have to tell you, I'm so happy that he is. I have really missed him the past few days. It would have been nice to have had someone to lean on right now."

"I have missed him too, if you want to know the truth. I love that boy like I do you. I know that sounds terrible, but he's so good for you, and Jordan just thinks the world of him." She looked at him with a sad smile. "I never had it in my head that you were a.... You know, son, I'm not sure what to call you that is correct. But I never knew that you were the way you are. I don't care. I might have several months ago. Aaron made it easier, I think. Me knowing that you met someone

134

that you can truly love and be loved back. You're loved as I always wanted you to be, and that makes it special for me. I suppose that's all I ever wanted for you. And just because Aaron is male too…well, I have come to the realization that love is love, no matter the form it comes to you in."

"Thank you, Mom. You have no idea how much that means to me." She kissed him on the cheek as she stood up. "This year Aaron and I are hosting Thanksgiving Day here. We're going to make it an all-day event, then on the Saturday after, get the houses ready for Christmas. Jake and Forrest were going to do it, but with Jake being the interim judge and Forrest having to do all the cases they have alone, they think it might be better this way. I asked if Cam and Rick wanted to, and it seems that Rick hasn't ever had this sort of thing—his parents weren't into it—and neither Emmi nor Cattie want to have to deal with the cooking and clean up, so it's coming here."

"What makes you think I want to deal with it either, young man?" He handed her the list of caterers that could and would do it. "Why don't you want me to cook it for us?"

"Because, my dear mother, I'd very much like for you and Howie to be able to sit at the table with us while we eat and enjoy our extended family. And I have another suggestion for you. I think you should make an honest man of poor Howie. If he was any more in love with you, I'd have to buy him a wheelbarrow to carry around the slobber he has when you're in the room with him."

"Brody Downs. What a thing to say to your mother." She reached into her pocket and showed him the ring when she put it on. "Howie proposed to me last night. I was trying to work in telling you between all the crap that has been going on."

"Yes, it has been a lot of crap over the last few days. And

we still have to deal with the next trial. Mom, I'm so happy for you and Howie. We'll have to get us another butler because he'll be my stepdad — finally — and I will not have him serving me. Promise me you'll talk to him." Mom said he was right and that she would. "I know we don't have to be a part of the trial for Emmi and the other women, but I'd very much like to be there if I can support them the way that they have me. All of us. I guess it's been postponed for a day, to get things cleared away for Jake. Who would have thought that Judge Bask would do that to him?"

"I did." Brody asked her how she knew. "The old codger knew what he was going to do. Just three days ago he was hinting around that he wanted to retire, and everyone in the diner told him that Jake should take his position. Then he asked me right out if I knew where he'd gone to college. All I had to do was mention that he was Jenna's grandson, and he told me that he'd completely forgotten that. She'd always been Ms. Jenna to him."

"I wondered about that. The man didn't even say a word about it when we got to the hospital, other than to say he was glad that I was there." Brody looked at his mom. "I was played right along with it, wasn't I?"

"I'd say you were." She was laughing when she stood up. "Brody, you will have a talk with Jordan, won't you? I just worry about him. I don't think he knows what to feel."

Brody sat there a bit longer. He wasn't really thinking of anything in particular, just letting his mind hit on one thing after another. What he needed to get from the grocery. That he was out of shaving cream. And when he realized that he was hungry, he could smell the bacon frying in the kitchen. Heading there, he saw Grandda and Jordan coming down the stairs.

"Jordan, how are you?" He said he was better now. "I'm

glad. Sometimes just having someone to talk to does the trick. I'm betting that your talk with Grandda was much nicer than the one that Grandma and I had. She's a little on the mean side."

"But she loves you." He said she did at that. "Grandda and Grandma are going to get married. And Grandma wants me to give her away. She told me that she could get Cam to do it, but he was going to be best man to Grandda. And Aunt Cattie is going to be her best maid. Isn't that cool?"

"Yes it is. And it's maid of honor, not best maid, I think." Jordan told him that was what Grandda wanted to call her. "Well, I think that's a great title then. You do know that you have to wear a tux, don't you? No jeans and T-shirts, I'm afraid."

"I know." He looked crestfallen for all of a second. "But I get to dance with all the pretty aunts and stuff. Grandda said they'll think me too handsome to just sit like a flower."

They were still laughing as they entered the kitchen. And standing there, literally with his hat in his hand, was Aaron. Rushing to him, Brody kissed him all over his face, telling him that he was so glad to see him. And when they sat down to breakfast, Aaron held his hand under the table and told them that it was over for him. He was done working where it took him away from the house so much. Brody felt better, like he was able to see the light at the end of the tunnel. Finally.

# Chapter 10

Aaron was sort of half listening to what everyone was saying about the last few days. It sounded to him like he should have come home earlier. But he was here now, and that was all that mattered. His boss was none too happy with him, but this was where he needed to be. Here, with his family.

Not just for Brody either. His sister needed him as much as he needed her. They were going through a great deal, the two of them, and he didn't know how well they'd be doing if not for the rest of them around them.

After things were cleaned up, he and Brody went to the living room. Brody had told him that it was fast becoming his favorite part of the house. Upon entering the big room with the fire place running, he could see why. It wasn't just a room, it seemed to be a cozy retreat.

"It's not really necessary for the fire to be running if you're too warm." Aaron said that he was fine and that he liked it. "I've missed you. I don't mean because all this shit is going on. We talked enough for you to know what was happening most of the time. No, I just missed having you around. Someone that I can physically lean into."

"I know just what you mean." To prove his point, Aaron pulled Brody over so that he was leaning his back into his chest. "I missed this a great deal. We were just getting used to touching each other. You know, like a loving couple."

"My mom told me that we should try really hard to show Jordan what a relationship is. A good one, she said. I agree with her. And Willy and Ann are tying the knot soon as well. With all this love and happiness, he's bound to have a better view of a relationship than he had with his mom and me. Anything is better than that one, I think."

They laughed, then just sat quietly again. Aaron thought of being a fulltime dad to Jordan. A house husband, he thought it might be called. He also thought of the position that he had been offered at the university to come in once a month and give some lectures on saving the planet, as well as the other creatures that were around us. He told Brody his plans about being there.

"I'd love that. And I know that Jordan would as well. Before I forget to tell you, there are papers you have to sign at the courthouse. It's just saying that you and I are going to have shared custody of Jordan. It says because my new job is a bit more dangerous, but that's not wholly it." Aaron thanked Brody and kissed him on the back of the neck. "We're not alone in the house, you know. And you make me scream like a little girl. I'm just saying."

The door opened then, and Mom came to the living room doorway to tell them they were all going out for a few hours. Jordan needed boots and she needed a thicker coat. As soon as the door closed behind them, he looked at Brody.

"I'll race you upstairs."

When Brody took off like a blast, Aaron sat there and laughed. Getting up, he started for the stairs to be with Brody. He felt good. Wonderful, actually, and things were coming together for them. Aaron loved his new family.

Brody was naked when he got to the bedroom. Not just naked, but he was stone hard and sliding his hand up and down his cock. Aaron watched him, his own cock starting to thicken in his pants as he stroked his fingers over it through his pants.

"I was wondering when you were going to get here." Aaron took off his shirt and then reached for the buttons on his pants. Brody watched him, his eyelids getting heavier and his breaths getting shorter. "I've thought of nothing else but having you suck my cock while I sucked yours. It's been all I could do to only jerk off once a day instead of all day long."

"I had to a couple of times as well. It was wonderful to just pull out my cock and let the cool breeze roll over it. Then when I was coming, just to be able to spray my cum all over the plants in front of me was almost too much." Brody moaned. "We'll have to do that when the weather turns warm again. Go out and jerk off on each other. Christ, just thinking about it has me nearly ready to run out there now."

"I think you'd lose your stiffness if you did it today. It's only forty. I know that might sound warm to some, but yesterday it was eighty-four. This weather is insane." Aaron joined him on the bed, both of them naked now and hard enough to hammer nails. "If you touch me, Aaron, I'm going to come right away."

It was tempting to make him come and then enjoy him all over. But he was needy too, and laid down on the bed with him. They were forever trying new things, the two of them. And they'd been watching videos about male to male sex. They were both excited to go to the next level of having sex.

Brody moved around so that Aaron's cock was in Brody's face. Christ, he was trembling with the need to just ram his cock in his mouth. Instead of ending this all too soon, Aaron wrapped his hand around Brody's cock, and nearly bit down when his own cock was in a warm wet place.

His cock was being abused, but in such a wonderful way. He wanted to stay like he was forever, but knew that he'd die if he did. Brody was getting really good at sucking him off. And Aaron decided that he was going to show his man that he could be just as consuming.

Taking Brody's cock into his mouth, Aaron moaned at the taste. There were enough juices on Brody's cock that Aaron felt like he could make a meal. As he bobbed over his lover's cock, he kept getting sidetracked in his work when Brody would do something more, giving his balls a slight twist, his cock a squeeze when he didn't expect it. Over and over he tortured him, so much so that Aaron kept forgetting the wonderful treat he had in front of him.

Brody was fucking his mouth over and over. It was amazing how much thicker and longer Brody's cock was than his own. But they both were well endowed. And Aaron was going to enjoy every inch of him.

Moving to another position, Aaron said that he wanted to fuck Brody. When they were in position, Brody down on his hands and knees in front of him, Aaron behind him. holding his aching cock in his hand, he slowly entered Brody's tight hole and felt sweat roll down his back, trying his best not to slam forward hard and come. Christ, this was harder than he'd thought. Only in the sense that he didn't know if he could hold out much longer.

"Take me. For Christ's sake, take me before I die here."

That was all he needed to hear, and Aaron did what his body told him. Slamming forward, he came hard, his body jerking hard at the release. And when Brody cried out too, Aaron reached down to help him by sliding his hand over his cock using his own juices.

142

Neither of them moved. Aaron wasn't even sure that he wanted to. His hands and knees were shaking so hard that he wasn't sure that he was going to be able to move once he fell in the bed. And when he laid down, taking Brody with him, the two of them laid there trying to catch their breaths. Aaron asked him if he was all right.

"Are you kidding? Christ, a couple of times I thought I was going to expire from the pleasure. And when you came? Aaron, I could have sworn that I could taste you in my mouth, it was so amazing." He turned around and kissed him, and Aaron kissed him back. "Living with you, I might have to eat more calories. I think that must have burned off about a thousand. I love you, Aaron. So much."

After showering along with playing around in the shower, the two of them set to work. Aaron was going to do some research on the college, and Brody said that he had some paperwork that he was filling out for the job with the police.

"I've decided that I'm going to take the university job." Brody asked him what had changed his mind. "I wasn't sure that I wanted to commit myself to anything at the moment. I mean, I would like to settle in here. Find my way around being with a family. And my whole life, I wanted to learn to cook. I can, but I mean like specialty meals that take all day to fix."

"Howie and Mom are getting married. Did I tell you that? Perhaps we can find us a cook that wants to work part time. Howie and my mom are going to travel some. Neither of them have done much of that before. Or do you want to take some classes first? I took a couple in college, and I rather enjoyed them." Aaron said that's what he was thinking. "Then do it. We have a very long time to get to do a lot of things now that we might not have had before. Take the classes. And if you are going to work at the university, your classes would be easier to get into, I would think."

The kitchen was just filling up with their families. Aaron had started calling Williemae Mom, and he noticed that Brody was calling Howie Dad. It was coming together, he thought. Just perfectly. The groceries were put away, and Jordan showed him the new boots he had gotten. Mom asked if they were hungry, and they were both starved. It had been a few hours since they'd eaten, and they had burned off a lot of energy. Setting up the line for everyone to make their own sandwich, Mom got out some soup that had been brought over by one of the locals to eat.

"I never thought of the good food people would be bringing us in light of the death in the family. Perhaps we can share it with Rachel's parents." Mom looked at him with a sweet smile. "That was very nice of you, Aaron, to have helped them get a place of their own. And Brody, you were a good son-in-law to them by letting them furnish it with the necessities. I'm to understand they were extremely grateful for it all."

"Brody and I spoke a few times on the phone while I was gone, and we talked about how much they've lost in this as well. It was nothing for me to help Brody find a house for them to live in. It's not huge—a couple of bedrooms—but the best part is, David has stopped drinking." Brody winked at him as he continued. "I do think that Emmi had a little to do with that. She is learning all kinds of things with her new gifts. And keeping David from making a fool of himself nightly was a good one. For everyone."

Jordan volunteered to call them. Aaron was shocked. He didn't think that Jordan's other grandparents had a lot to do with him over the years. But when he got off the phone, he looked at Aaron.

"I've decided that they need me, Dad." Then he moved

144

into the dining room to help his grandma set the table.

Aaron wondered if he'd heard him right. Jordan had just called him Dad, he thought. Looking at Brody, he saw the biggest smile on his face, and he patted him on the back.

"Welcome to fatherhood, Aaron. Ain't it the best thing ever?"

Aaron nodded. Christ, he was a dad. Jordan had called him Dad.

Going into the dining room, Aaron couldn't help it. He picked Jordan up and hugged him tightly to his body.

"I love you too, Dad. Thank you for making my dad so happy."

The hug lasted for so long that Aaron didn't want to let the little boy go. When he pulled back enough to look at him, Jordan smiled at him.

"You make me happy too. Can I have a puppy?"

~*~

Fred was just biding his time in the jail. Never without a plan, he was playing around with several opportunities as he sat there. The women that worked here, they'd be good candidates for his next woman. But he knew that when he left here, he was going to have to lay low or move on. And for right now, the option of moving on, he thought, was his best bet.

The meals came and went three times a day. He'd only partake of the drinks when they were offered. It wasn't that he wasn't hungry—he just didn't trust that they wouldn't try something on him. It had happened to him before. Once when he'd been in an institution, they'd done all sorts of things to him.

Fred remembered that time. He also remembered the person who had signed him into such a place. His mother had thought him to be a deviant, and had decided that since

145

he couldn't keep his dick in his pants, he would have to suffer for it. And suffer he did.

They had started with whippings. All that had done to the sixteen-year-old boy was scar up his back until he was ashamed to remove his shirt around anyone. Then when that had no effect whatsoever, they'd tried to get into his head.

Not only did that not work for them, but it also showed him that he was a good deal smarter than the men that were with him. The so-called doctors would be astonished with some of his questions and answers, so much so that they'd walk away shaking their heads at his brilliance. From then on they would try and trip him up. Two people would talk and the third one would be measuring his brain waves. They'd never let him see his records, but Fred didn't need to see them to know that he had a high IQ. And he'd been using his intelligence since he'd escaped to have fun.

But, before he could get away, his mother had them perform a nasty surgery on him, cutting into his dick until it only worked to piss out of. And sometimes, at first, he'd have to have someone catheterize him just to give him relief. Now he did it all on his own, and didn't have to waste his time with any more fools and idiots.

When he left here, he knew the first thing he was going to have to do was get rid of all the stash he had. The cars would have to go first, then all the collections that he'd gathered. No one would ever find them, mostly because he had them in a very special place that no one would think to look.

When the next meal was brought to him, Fred noticed that there were two bottles of water rather than just the one. Sipping the water, telling himself it was a fine meal, he wondered about Emmi. The woman hadn't been that beautiful when he'd first approached her. He would have made a few more trips to her home if she had been. But she'd disappeared, he remembered. And without a forwarding address.

Laughing at his own joke, he looked up when someone said his name. Another thing to add to his list was how had someone had found out his real name. He asked the nicely dressed woman what she wanted.

"I'm here to figure out what sort of things you wish to use to save yourself." Fred told her that he didn't need her services. "I'm sorry, Mr. Simmons, but I was told that under no circumstances am I to allow you to dismiss me. They are not allowing for you to call for a mistrial if things do not go your way."

"And they are so sure that they're going to go their way?" The woman just stared at him. "You have the face of an attorney, I'm sorry to say. But it matters little to me how much you try and hide your thoughts. I'm capable of reading your face regardless. They think they have enough evidence to prove something, do they? It's doubtful that this will get past the initial stages. And if it does, then it'll only take me that much longer to get what I want."

"And what is that?" Fred gave her back the same look. "Ah, so you think you can pull a rabbit out of the hat, do you? It's very doubtful that you will walk out of here a free man, from what I've heard. Because this is more than just criminal charges of B&E against you. That's why I'm to stay at your side."

"If the taxpayers wish to waste money on your services, which I have said I do not require, then that's fine with me." He stood up, stretching as he did so. "I don't suppose you play chess, do you? It would help the time pass if you did. Do they teach women that nowadays?"

"Yes, my brother taught me. And I do have a nice set, as a matter of fact." She asked if she may return with it. "And while we play, I can pick your mind, if that's all right with

147

you. I mean, even if you don't want me around, having more information can't hurt anyone, can it?"

"No. I suppose not. And when you return, young lady, I'd like to see your identification. You can't be too careful when you're in this sort of situation." The woman, he didn't remember her name right at the moment, told him that she'd be back soon. Fred sat back down on the cot and sipped the water again.

People were playing right into his hands. The woman had said that she'd pick his brain, but it was going to be the other way around. By the time the game had stretched out as long as he could make it, giving her the illusion that she was a good player, he'd have every trick in the book that they knew. None of them, and especially this woman, was as smart as he was.

When the woman returned she was no longer dressed in a suit, but in jeans and a pretty floral shirt. He had just finished using the commode. His groin hurt, his dick rubbed raw from the pants he had been forced to wear. But as soon as she pulled out the magnificent set, Fred would gladly have turned over the keys to his mind for a chance to play on it.

She was pulling out the pieces—white was a polished ivory—when he realized this was better than he could have imagined. The detail was exquisite, the pieces all signed on the bottom by an artist that had been dead longer than the woman and he had been living. But when she paused before pulling out the black pieces, she started putting them away.

"What is this? Teasing a man after showing him this lovely set?" She said that she'd forgotten her identification in her haste to return. "No, no. We'll play. Then tomorrow, if you still wish to sit here and lose, you can bring it then. Please, lay it out for me. I wish to see it."

The darker pieces were all made of mahogany. Christ,

they too were well polished. The heads of them were just slightly worn from being picked up and moved. Fred had never seen such a set, and he wondered where she'd gotten it. Asking her, he couldn't believe her answer.

"My grandda gave it to me. Actually, I think I remember winning it from him. But as his eyesight was failing, he told me to take it as a prize for sitting with him all the time. My brother and I, we play when we can. But I've recently married, so I'm teaching my husband how to play. He's good, but he lacks the discipline to be great yet." He asked if she taught him with this set. "Yes. A game is meant to be played, my grandda said. And if you only save the special for special occasions, you might not remember that it's there. This one sets out all the time so we can play when we want. It's my favorite pastime."

Fred wanted to bargain with her, but decided that would show his hand in how much he liked the set. He was just greedy enough to play with her set in saying that they'd play two games, one of each color.

As soon as the game began, Fred realized that she was no mere player, she was good. They played for several hours. Her laughter rang down the otherwise empty halls. When she won, she didn't gloat. And when she lost—which wasn't all that often, as much as he hated to admit, even to himself—she didn't whine or cry either.

They talked, mostly about the game, her grandfather, and some things of her life. Never once did she ask him about the upcoming trial. She didn't pound him for any clues. They just sat and played until his dinner tray came.

"I have to get going." Fred actually hated for her to leave him now that he'd found someone that he could enjoy. "I guess we have a big day tomorrow. I'll be there, but I don't think you'll need anything I have to offer."

She put out her hand, and before he could think that it might be a bad idea, Fred was shaking her hand back. All he felt was warmth from her. That and the softness of a female. When she was finished packing up the set, he asked her finally for her name.

"I'm sorry. I could have sworn— Never mind. I'm Cattie. Cattie Huffman." She smiled at him, blinding him for a moment. "I'll see you tomorrow, Fred. And thanks so much for the games."

When she was gone, he sat back on the cot. It had never felt this lonely in here before. He'd had his thoughts and plans, but now, he felt almost like he'd lost something with her gone. Lying back on the little bed, he wondered if he'd look for her when this was all finally over. Then he decided that he'd not. She was special, Cattie Huffman, and he'd allow her to live out her days without him intruding on her life.

The rest of his evening was planning out his tomorrow. After the trial he'd have to hide out, and he figured that he'd just go to his hideaway and stay there for a while. No one knew about the place, so he'd be free to clean up his things. And he'd have to make a trip to the cemetery to gather his trophies, as the police would call them.

No one had ever suspected that he'd taken anything. Not a piece of jewelry for him. No little mementos that he'd have to keep in a box, or in his case a large bag. Fred was smart in what he took. A single pubic hair, just one, that he plucked out of her pussy so that he could have it to look at later. Fred had them all laminated, with their names on each little hair, and dated. Anytime he wanted, he'd just pull one out and remember what fun he'd had.

Killing his mother hadn't been hard for him to do. He had no remorse for killing her. He didn't feel like he'd owed her anything for bringing him into the world. Nor did he think she'd gotten more than she deserved. She had ruined him, as easily as if she had plunged the blade into his dick herself.

When the lights were turned off, he got up to use the bathroom again. He'd almost waited too long to go, not wanting the young Cattie to leave his company just yet. Pulling out his scarred and ruined dick, he looked down at it, remembering like it was yesterday waking up to find it like it was and his mother standing over him.

"You will not touch yourself again, Fredrick. Do you hear me? No more beating that thing with your hands and my Vaseline so that you can wave that nasty thing out in the wind." Fred asked her what she'd done. "I did? I did nothing to you but bring you here so that you could be taken care of. And they've done it. They had to if they wished to be paid. And you'll be a eunuch now, never to be able to play with it for the rest of your days."

She left him there. His own mother had had him hurt badly, then she'd left, telling him as she laughed that she never wanted to see him darken her door again. And that if she even heard of him coming around her home, she'd do worse to him than she'd paid the surgeon to do, and without putting him to sleep first.

It had taken him nearly a month to be able to get around on his own, but he'd been stuck with the bag at his side for a lot longer than that. He worked at it, making himself pee when he felt the urge. But there were times, in the beginning, that he had to have help. It only took him a few days and many tries to understand how to do that personal thing to himself.

After he'd escaped, killing the surgeon, nurse, and anyone else that got in his way, Fred didn't so much as peek his head out of his hiding space for three months. Food wasn't all that hard to come by, not when he had his uncle's gun and plenty of ammo. And there were enough apples and other fruit in the trees surrounding the place that he ate well during that time. And he got stronger.

Chopping wood that he didn't need made his upper body stone hard. Walking everywhere, even when the pain was too much, gave him endurance. And then when he was as fit as he could be, he snuck into his mother's home, cutting her into small pieces with a chain saw. He smiled at her screams until she died, and then took everything that he could find — money, food, and her car — out of the place before heading back to the hideaway and waiting out the backlash from her death.

Fred was not just a careful man, but he didn't kill anymore, not unless they touched him. Then he would quickly take care of their remains and go on as if nothing had happened. His life, as far as he was concerned, was about as perfect as he could have wished for.

# Chapter 11

Aaron didn't have much knowledge about being an attorney. He had one, of course, but he didn't use him all that much. What he did understand was that this trial was going to be a slam dunk, Forrest said, and he was thrilled to death to be there for it.

Because of their relationship, Forrest had had to step down as the attorney for Emmi. It didn't bother him that much, he told them, but he had been worried about things not going the way that he wanted. Then Cam stepped up.

"I have a doctorate in law." Everyone looked at the young man, then he smiled. "I have a lot of degrees, really, but I think this one might be able to help us all. Especially Emmi. Since we're not at all related, I can represent her. And while a lot of people know that we're all friends, Fred does not. And Cattie said that she'd sit way in the back, and since her name is different than mine now too, we should be safe."

But just to be sure, they ran it all through Samuel Bask, including how they'd found out most of the information that they now had. By the time they were finished, the man was regretting not being in on this one. He was nearly giddy with excitement for them.

"You guys need to be in business for yourself on this. I mean, I don't think they had this much information when someone was shot and they saw the man do it. Holy smokes, gentlemen, you are seriously going to blow this sucker out of the water." To keep things really on the up and up, Jake wasn't at this meeting. In fact, they didn't even tell him about it. "I'm retiring. Don't tell my buddy Jake yet. I'm sure he's going to be doing a good job, and I just don't have any heart in it anymore."

"I'm sure that once Jake starts to settle into his job, which even you have to admit hasn't been an easy transition, he'll do much better. But I must tell you, I think he's figured out that you fooled him." Samuel laughed with the rest of them when Forrest spoke. "He's loving the perks too, that you set up for him. His grandma, she'd be happy, I think."

Aaron knew for a fact that she was happy. Jenna was there now with them, and she was having a good time telling them to tell the judge that she was. The man had been sweet on her, but Aaron didn't find that surprising. It seemed to him that everyone had been sweet on the woman. And those that weren't had hated her with a passion that held no bounds, her son one of them.

The rest of the afternoon was spent at the house. They were still ordering things to fill it out; many of the rooms had sat empty for some time. So they were also having the walls painted, as well as any plumbing work done that needed to be updated. Paying Jake and Forrest to buy the house made him feel better. Renting wasn't that bad, he supposed, since he'd known that he was going to own it eventually, but ownership was better.

Brody was having a clinic put in at home. That way if there was an emergency with the pack or one of them, he could easily take care of it there rather than having to go all the way to the hospital.

Aaron was enjoying his time settling in as a house husband. So far he'd taken a few cooking classes, and was having a great time with those. And Howie was having fun showing him how to cook things too. Who knew that chopping an onion could be so messy and a blast as well?

Jordan was settling in well. With his mother gone, the boy had seemed to relax a great deal. Walking to the library when he wanted. Making friends with the neighborhood children. They were mostly shifters of one kind or another, but that didn't seem to matter to him. Children had the least amount of prejudice of any people he knew when it came to making friends, and Aaron thought that everyone could learn from them.

The phone was ringing as he entered the kitchen at lunchtime. After saying his name, he waited for someone to speak. When there didn't seem to be anyone there, he hung up. Halfway to the sink to wash up to make a salad, it rang again. He thought it was a wrong number, so said just his last name this time.

"Dad?" Aaron held tightly to the counter when he told Jordan it was him. "I'm at my regular school now, and they want to speak to you and Dad. I don't want to be here anymore. Can I go back to my other school?"

They'd moved him to the local school when his mother was no longer a threat. Aaron and Brody both thought that the move would be better, as it was closer to home too.

"Are you all right, son?"

Jordan started crying, and Aaron reached for his coat as he tried to get him to tell what had happened. Cattie walked in with Tyson just as he started speaking again.

"They want you to come here because my teacher is saying

that I'm a degenerate. And that you and Dad are sick-o's. Dad, I'm so sorry. I didn't do anything." He asked him where the teacher was now. "She's in the classroom. I'm not allowed to return because of you and Dad. I don't understand."

"You wait right there, Jordan. I'm coming. Is there anything in the room that is yours?" He said that she'd boxed it up. "I see. I'm coming. I'm sorry, but this isn't going to be pretty, son. All right? I don't want to embarrass you, but—"

"Dad, just come and get me, please? I don't want to be in her room no more. She made me feel really bad because you and Dad love each other." Aaron told Jordan he was coming. "All right. I love you, Dad."

After telling him he loved him, Aaron hung up and had to stand there for several minutes just breathing. Cattie asked him where Brody was. Aaron really wished he was there, but he was in surgery right now.

"I'm coming with you then." Cattie sat on the chair after pouring herself some tea, but Tyson looked as fired up as he was. Not that Cattie wasn't, but she was letting the two of them handle things. "There are laws that prohibit that. I wonder if she's aware of how many of them she broke. And she singled out my nephew. That is not going to happen. Also, I'm calling in Jake and Forrest. Hell, they'll all want to be in on this. Damn it all to fucking hell."

By the time Aaron, Tyson, and Cattie were pulling into the school parking lot, not only were Forrest and Jake there, but so were all the other men. Quincey was there, as well as Scott. This woman was in for a rare treat, Aaron thought with a grin.

As soon as he walked into the principal's office, she laughed. Mrs. Hersey had an idea that Ms. Adams had bitten off more than she could chew today. And when she asked them to follow her to the conference room, several more teachers came in to join them. All of them, it seemed, had heard what was said to little Jordan Downs. Brody showed up just as the teacher joined them in the room.

"Just one more moment, please." Mrs. Hersey said that one more person was joining them.

Ms. Adams was looking like she'd won already. Her face was pinched up, and she had a glint in her eye that told Aaron that it didn't matter what was said in here, she wasn't going to back off. The school superintendent, Mr. Donald Black, showed up and sat in the back of the room without anyone seeing him. Aaron nodded at him and he put his finger to his lips. Aaron was just fine with that too.

"I'm here to talk to you about my son and something you said to him — "

"You can beg me all you want to take him back in my room, but I won't do it. I have rights just as much as he does." Aaron said that wasn't why he was there. "I don't even want that child in this school, to be honest with you. He's living with two men that are sleeping together. That's a sin."

"To you." She told Aaron it was to most people. "So you say. But you can't say those things to him in front of his classmates. You're making him a target when you — "

"You made him a target when you started having relations with another man, you pervert. And having all these other 'friends' in here with you? It just shows how many of you perverts there are in this town. Had I known there were this many faggots around here, I swear to you that I'd never have taken this job."

She sat down with a flounce. That's all Aaron could call it, and he sat up straighter in his chair. He'd only been a pervert, as she called him, for a short time, but he'd been around the world and back to know that this woman wasn't really any different than most when it came to homosexuality.

157

"You don't have to take him back in your class, Ms. Adams. I just want you to apologize to—"

"No. That's not going to happen either. I know my rights, and I won't—"

"If you cut me off again, I'm going to press charges against you for being prejudiced against my son." She opened her mouth again while starting to stand. Aaron had had enough. Slamming both his hands down on the tabletop, he shouted in a roaring voice at her, "Sit down and shut up!"

The room snickered, and he looked around at them all. It was now as quiet as a church in the room, and he stood up beside Forrest and Jake. She was going to get a lesson in what the perverts did for her before she even opened her first book this school year.

"You will find that we're just people like you are." She shook her head, but didn't get up or say anything this time. "We love each other forever. And we raise our children in the same manner that you would. Jordan is a good kid. Smart, and loves both of us very much. You've, by your own voice, made the other children, who were accepting of both him and us, think about what we are. By you saying those things in your class, where others could hear you, you've given them voices that they hadn't formed yet. By you pointing out that Jordan is different for having two men love him, he can be bullied. You, yourself, have bullied him. As well as showed the other children that it's all right to do what you do, no matter how wrong it is.

"Jake and Forrest are also perverts, as you call them. Jake is a judge of the county, Forrest an attorney. This school year they donated the funds for the new teachers' lounge that you have. As well as the garden that is being put in behind the school that is just for teachers to go to." Aaron went to stand behind Cam and Rick as he continued to tell her what she was

158

saying was hurting only herself. "Cameron is an FBI agent that is running the local offices right now. Doing a great job of it too. Rick is an author. His first book is going to be made into a movie. Their money bought gift cards for each teacher this year, in the amount of five thousand dollars each. That doesn't include the items that Cam's sister, a cop, as well as her husband Tyson, a cop as well, donated for the teachers to use every day. Crayons and paper, tissues, as well as glue and other supplies, so that you'd have them and the teachers wouldn't have to use the gift card for anything but making the rooms brighter and more enjoyable for you to use."

He went down the line to each of them there that had come together in one way or another to make the school much better funded, as well as a clean place to be daily. When he stood behind Brody, he put his hands on his shoulders.

"Brody is a doctor. One that donates his time to come in each week to make sure that the students are healthy enough to come to class. He brings in toothbrushes for them that he gets wholesale, as well as toothpaste for them. Both he pays for." She smirked at him. "I work for the government. I go out, take pictures and other things of animals that we once thought extinct. I have also arranged, with the principle as well as the superintendent, to have a week in the summer that kids will get a chance for one on one time to be up close and personal with some of these animals. To mention only a few, we're having a giraffe brought in. A lioness and her cubs, as well as a rhino. They'll be well supervised, as will the children. We, perverts as you called us, have made your job as a teacher much better than anywhere else in the state."

Aaron sat down. After telling her how much they'd done for her and her students, he'd not been able to change her mind. He could see it by the look on her face.

"Are you finished now? Am I allowed to speak?" She

stood up, her face tighter than before, her hatred there for everyone in the room with them to see. "I am so happy that you told me what you gave the school. I won't use them. The money that I have used for the room, I'll repay you for it. You're not welcome in my world, so you won't be in it, and that child that you're raising to be just like you won't be either. What if, God forbid, he grows up to be just like all of you? You sicken me. I won't use anything that you've touched and tainted with your unholiness."

"You're right about that, Ms. Adams." The superintendent stood up then, and Ms. Adams started falling all over herself to be next to him. "I think, in the words of Aaron here, I'd like for you to sit down and shut up."

The words were softly said. The tone was normal. But it was no less demanding than when Aaron had said it. And when Ms. Adams sat down, Aaron could see fear replacing her confidence. Mr. Black leaned to Mrs. Hersey and whispered in her ear. When she got up to leave, the room seemed to have tightened up with the tension.

"Ms. Adams, you're fired. And before you say another word, I want you to know that I had another background check of you come across my desk not long ago. For whatever reason, we took your word with the one you handed us when you were hired. Thanks to you, we'll be doing a much better job from now on." He handed the single sheet to Aaron. "You'd be amazed at the things you can find out if you know just where to look. This is the fourth school that you've been fired from in the last year. And in those firings, you were also arrested for causing a riot in your room. Bullying four of your students, as well as burning a chair that one of the students that you had in your room sat in. I'm assuming that you thought his parents were deviants as well."

"You cannot be taking their side in all this. I'm a normal

human, and they're...well, they're monsters." Mr. Black said that the only monster in the room was her. Cattie came in the room behind Ms. Adams but said nothing. And neither did the rest of the room. "I have the right to not have children in my room that are disruptive and rude to me. And the very idea of him being in the same room with other, normal people makes me ill."

"You do have that right, at that. But since I also have rights, the right to terminate your services, that won't be a problem for you, now will it?" Other officers came in the room, each of them in assault gear, all of them holding rifles. "Your things are being packed up now. Your class is going to be taken over by another teacher, and you will be escorted out of here."

Before anyone could guess what the police and armed guards were there for, Ms. Adams jumped from her seat and pulled out a gun. But before she could fire it on anyone but the ceiling, she was taken to the table and her gun tossed across the room. Christ, Aaron hadn't thought that guns were allowed on the school grounds, much less in the classroom. Then something else occurred to him, and he had to sit down.

"You all right?" Aaron nodded, and had to put his head down between his legs. Brody asked him again, this time laughing a little. "Are you really all right?"

"She could have killed Jordan." Brody said that he'd thought of that too when Cattie called him. "She knew what Ms. Adams was going to do? Did she tell you to come here in case someone was hurt?"

"Yes, to both questions. I was finishing up anyway, and decided that I'd come home when I got a call from Cattie. As you can well imagine, I was scared out of my boxers too." Aaron sat up. "You gave a good speech. And I think you impressed the rest of them too. Not that I think it did her a bit of good, but it was a good one. And Mr. Black, he hadn't

161

realized that we'd done so much for this district."

"I hadn't meant to do that for him to know. I wanted her to know what she was going to be giving up if she decided to pursue this about Jordan." They watched as she was dragged out of the room, screaming about perverts the entire time. "I've seen people like her everywhere I've been."

"I have as well. It's sad that people don't just mind their own business." Aaron said that he thought that people would get along better if there were less homophobic people in the world. "I have to agree with you there too, I'm afraid. How about we just go home? Jordan is going to meet us there. He and Cam were going to have some lunch. He said he needed to talk to him anyway."

"What do you suppose about?" Brody said that he didn't care so long as he was home soon, and that he got to go home and take a nap. "Yes, I forgot that you left the house before dawn this morning. Everything turn out all right?"

"Yes, thankfully. The mother had a seven-pound little girl, and both are doing fine." They walked to Aaron's car, as Brody had walked to the school. "We're going to have to get us a better car for winter. I'd forgotten how much the weather can change on a dime around here."

They talked about the weather. Yesterday it had been nearly seventy out. Today the high was only going to be forty. Ohio weather was as ever-changing as a mood, Aaron told Brody. Today cold, tomorrow who knew what the weather was going to hold for the state.

When they were home finally, they did just what they said they would and sat out on the deck until the sun going down necessitated them going in for warmer weather. Then, they both sat in their recliners and took a long, much needed nap.

~*~

Jordan had sixty dollars to spend, and he thought that it was important that his dads knew that he loved them both. Today, they'd not asked him to back down or to run away. His friend from the pack told him that his parents were very brave to stand up against humans about their friendship and love, because humans, to him, were very rude. Not only that, but they weren't as accepting as shifters were. He wasn't sure what all that meant, not really, but he knew that he loved them. And Cam was going to help him out.

"You think anything here is going to make it, buddy?" Jordan shook his head. "If you ask me, I think you're going about this all wrong. If I were your parents, I'd want you to just be glad that they have you."

"You're weird, Uncle Cam." They were both laughing when they started by the Christmas stuff. "I think that I should do what Uncle Rick said to do—get them a steak and let them cook out."

"That is what I'd want." Jordan eyed his uncle. "I told you before we left that I was starving, that I needed food. You said we'd find pretzels. Where are my pretzels, little man?"

Leaving the store for the mall, they talked about what his parents liked. And while Uncle Cam was driving, he said that his sister had said for Jordan to get them matching aprons, with their names on them.

"They'd like that. They're always spilling something on their shirts when they cook out." Jordan was warming to the idea. "And if I get one for Dad Brody that's for cooking out, and one for Dad Aaron that has a cake on it, they'd know which one was theirs. What do you think?"

It only took them about an hour to get the aprons made with their names on them. He thought that Dad Brody and Dad Aaron was perfect too. Jordan was even able to get them giftwrapped, and Uncle Cam got his pretzel. Cam said that he hoped someday that he and Rick had a kid that was nothing like Jordan, and Jordan laughed. He was teasing him, he knew—Jordan loved his uncles and aunts. On the way home, they stopped for cake and ice cream to go with dinner.

Jordan was excited, too, that he'd get to start new with a new school teacher. His mom was gone, and he had good parents. He did think about his mom; a great deal, as a matter of fact. And it made Jordan upset that he wasn't hurt that she had died. That she was gone forever.

She'd not been there for him, not even when he was sick or didn't feel good. They'd never done any of the things that she would promise him. He'd wanted to go to the movies with just her, like his friend Jason did. But she was too busy getting her hair or nails done. Jordan didn't tell anyone, but he'd not loved his mom for a long time. He'd not even liked her most of the time. And that made Jordan feel like he was missing something.

"Can I talk to you, Uncle Cam?" He told him that he could talk to him anytime. "I wanna talk to you about my mom."

He told him everything, things that he'd forgotten about until just then. About when Ralph had come to the house and she'd make Jordan stay in the kitchen. How Ralph had hurt him sometimes. Cam asked him questions too, and Jordan felt like he was really listening to him—just like his dads did.

"And when Ralph was hurting you, did he touch you in places that he shouldn't have." Jordan knew what he was asking, and told him no, never that. "Good. And you think you feel like you're missing something. Are you missing anything, Jordan? Didn't you give your mom every opportunity to have fun with you? Did you tell her that you wanted to do things?"

"Yes, all the time. But she didn't want me around. And I feel like I should be crying or something because she died." He asked him why he should do either of those things. "Because she was my mom and she died. When my dog was killed, I cried a lot."

"Jordan, you feel just like you want to feel, and no one around you is going to make you feel any different. You were hurt by her and Ralph. You are, even though I think you're the smartest five-year-old I know, only just a kid. She should have taken better care with her words, her love, and with you. But she didn't. And for that, she lost out."

Uncle Cam told him that today had marked a good starting point for him. The teacher coming from another district was already excited to teach all her students equally, and Uncle Cam said that she was a nice person as well as an accepting one. Jordan was going to do just what his uncle told him to do — wipe his mind clean of all the bad stuff, but learn from it and have a good life. He deserved it.

# *Chapter 12*

This was the third day of the trial, and Fred was thinking that he'd be out of here by the end of today, tomorrow at the latest. He'd not counted on so many of the women coming forward after what he'd done to them, and that had bothered him a bit. But since not one of them had seen him, nor did they really understand what had happened to them, he was just sitting in his chair enjoying the prosecutor making a fool of himself. A couple of times the idiot had asked him if he wanted to ask anything of the women.

"Ask them what, pray tell? I don't have any idea what you might be talking about with this parade of beautiful women. No, I have nothing to ask of them. Unless, of course, they'd like to have dinner with me some night." The room snickered, he thought. It couldn't have been them mumbling about how he was sick. No, that just wouldn't be something they'd do.

Fred wasn't a sick person. He was doing this because it was fun—and harmless. Oh yeah, he'd have a little sport in knocking them around. But he didn't think that was his fault. Not entirely. They should be more diligent, safe and aware in their surroundings. Then he thought of the woman—the

167

last one, Emmi. He'd been caught with her. And he'd been wondering for the last three days why she'd not been brought to the front like the others had.

Fred sat up straighter in his chair when a woman that he didn't know came to be sworn in. Once she was seated, he listened to the attorney for Emmi question the woman.

"She's been missing for a few months now. It was as if nothing had been taken from her room, and her car is missing along with her purse." He wondered who she might have been, this missing person. Fred was wondering if they were trying to pin unsolved murders on him that he'd had nothing to do with when she spoke again. "For a few days leading up to her disappearance, she was complaining of falling in her sleep. How her body was being abused, and that she had no any idea what was going on. Then one night, I was going to stay with her but I got the flu. That was the last time that I saw her."

"And did you search for her?"

If the girl answered him, Fred was no longer paying attention. He was thinking of the reasons. Of course she had looked for her friend, thought Fred, and he'd almost taken care of her too. Not as he had the girl. He didn't remember her, of course, or the dead woman. Because if she disappeared, then she'd touched him in some way. And if there was touching, then she was as good as dead.

Drifting mentally to his list, Fred thought about all the things he was going to have to do once he was set free. The first thing would have to be to take care of the cars and all the credit cards he'd accumulated. Then there was his stash. He'd have to pick it up. Not that he thought they'd ever be able to find it. He had a feeling that they'd not be able to find their way out of a wet paper bag without written instructions. Then there was the —

"Mr. Simmons, are you listening to me?" He looked around and saw that the entire courtroom was staring at him. Embarrassed to be caught unawares, he asked the man what it is he'd missed. "You're being called to testify on your own behalf."

He was? No one had told him this might come up. Then of course, he'd fired his attorney yesterday when all he was doing was doodling on his notepad and not saying a word. When he stood up, his legs shackled to the floor, an officer came to unhook him and then helped him to the big chair. After that, Fred was sworn in to tell the truth and blah blah blah.

Sitting down, he tried to look as beaten as he could. Fred knew that they'd looked up his medical record, and thought that had made them a little ill. Funny, he thought, all it had done for him when he'd seen himself was make him angry enough to seek revenge. And he had. But that had been another time and another Fred. This Fred liked to have fun, not kill unless necessary.

"Mr. Simmons, can you tell us why you were in the apartment of one Sarah Ross?" He didn't know her last name, or thought that he'd remembered it being something else, but he only stared at the man. Cameron Henderson wasn't getting crap out of him. "If you need a reminder, I'm sure that I can find the video that was taken that day. The one where you broke into the house and tied the young woman down after stripping her of her clothing. Does that ring a bell?"

"Can't say that it does. I think you might have the wrong man." Fred just stared at him then. He had this in the bag. "I just don't know what you're talking about, young man."

Playing stupid was his strong suit. He could play the smart man too when it was necessary. But today, he thought that he'd have better luck —

169

"I see. Then perhaps you can tell us about the property that is out in Ashland County. We found the records where your uncle on your mother's side is the owner. There are a great many cars there. What can you tell me about them?" He was slightly panicky, and he knew that a panicky man was a caught man. "Sir? If that is too much for you, perhaps you can tell me about the saw equipment out there, as well as the kiln that has been used recently."

Fred tried to think if he'd ever told a soul about that place. Even had someone meet him there, or even anyone follow him there. No, not anyone. Fred looked at the man, trying his best to think what else he might know.

*I know a great deal about you, Fred. Most of it is going to be shown here in the court room today.* Fred looked around—the man's voice was in his head. Looking at the judge, he asked him if he'd heard him, just to make sure.

"He asked you about the property in Ashland County, and the kiln and working equipment that was there. Are you going to answer him?"

Was he? No. Neither the voice in his head nor the one that everyone heard.

*Fred, are you afraid? You should be. I found your little stash. Very clever of you to put it upon your mother's grave. Right under the flower pot that sticks in the ground. Pubic hair. And guess what, it's covered in your prints.*

Fred was terrified of the voice. Looking around, he wondered what he could do, where he could go, when the voice spoke again.

*You killed your own mother? How very terrible of—*

"Your Honor, I think something is wrong." The man asked him what it could be, and reminded him once again that he'd not answered the questions. "Because he knows. There is a voice in my head that says everything. Where my

170

stash is and everything."

"What stash are you talking about?" He had to think. Did the man say he had them, or did he only say he knew where they were? "Mr. Simmons, you have been found competent to stand trial. What are you doing now?"

"I don't know."

He looked around over and over, trying to find a device that would be able to put out words when there wasn't anyone speaking. Fred bent his head down as far as he could, searching for something in his ears or around his head. Nothing. There wasn't any reason whatsoever that he was having this happen to him.

"I'd like to have a recess. I need a break for a moment. Something isn't right."

"I'm afraid that's not possible, Mr. Simmons. Mr. Henderson is asking you questions, and we're awaiting answers from you. Come now, answer the questions and we can call it a day, if you're still unsure of yourself." That sounded like a good plan. "Now, what were you talking about with a stash of some sort?"

*Do you think that you're imagining this? You're not. I'm really in your head, and I'm finding all sorts of evil deeds done by you. And the women? Well, you do that because you're unable to perform any other way.* He shouted at the man to shut up, but the judge and the attorney just stared at him. *Does it bother you when women look at your shriveled up dick and laugh? I bet they do that a great deal. Is that why you don't allow them to touch you? You said that it's because of DNA, but I know what it really is. You hurt badly when your shriveled dick gets —*

"Yes, that's why I break into their homes! Damn it, leave me alone!" Fred rubbed his face and apologized. "I'm having a rough time. Could I have the questions repeated to me?"

*Oh, you think that you're having a rough time now? No, you're*

171

*as good as cooked when you go to prison. Tell them it all, Fredrick Simmons. Tell them about how you are pained by the slightest bit of excitement. How it hurts you to even watch a porn movie, and that your mother had you done this way because you were forever whacking off in her underwear, her dirty underwear. That's what she called you, didn't she, Fredrick? Dirty boy Freddy.*

"No, you fool. Stop it. I killed my mother because she took me to that place, and they cut into my dick so that she could see if it was defective. And they ruined me." He looked at the judge again. "Make him stop. Please. Those things, he's telling stories that are mine, not his."

"I'm sorry, but I haven't any idea what you're talking about. And I'm going to find you in contempt if you do not cooperate and answer the questions, Mr. Simmons. When you said that you had no need for an attorney for this hearing, that did not allow you to not answer questions put to you just because you find them something that you don't want to tell him. Now, answer the questions." He tried to think what the questions might have been. "Sir, you're trying my patience right now."

*Answer him, Fredrick the dirty, and tell him what I know.* He told the voice to shut up. *But I cannot. I'm trying to get you to tell him where your stash is. Or do I have to make sure that he shows you what he's been able to dig up? I can do that. Is that what I can do — ?*

"I do not want you to tell anyone where my stash of trinkets is. Those are mine, not yours, and I'll have you know that you're to stay away from them." Someone asked him where they were. "You know. You told me. They're under my mother's headstone. All marked and ready for me to get when I get out of here."

He could no longer tell the voice in his head from the ones in the room. Every time he was asked a question or told

172

something, Fred would tell it whatever it wanted to know. He had a feeling that if he did that, it would leave him alone. But by the time the judge called lunch, he was exhausted from having question after question tossed at him. Every little thing seemed to be something else that he'd forgotten about.

He'd killed a cat when he was a child. The neighbor had one; he was not allowed to because of the allergies that his mother had. She was forever making his life hell. So Fred had taken the cat and hidden it away. Putting it under a bucket with a brick on the top was the only place that he could find when the cat came into his yard. Then, after several days, he realized that he'd forgotten about it. By then it was stiff as a board, and had small white worms crawling all over it.

Then there was the time that he'd gotten in the school bus yard and had sugared all the gas tanks. His mother had been so angry at him for that. School had been canceled for a month, and he'd been stuck at home with her. Other things too, little and large times he'd let his meanness, as his mother called it, free.

When he was taken to the van to eat with the chains on, he didn't have the energy. His body felt beaten, his groin like he'd been fiddling with himself again. When he tried to eat, all he could manage was a few bites before he laid down and closed his eyes. Fred didn't want to go back, but he knew that he had to get a handle on himself.

Then there was what he'd told the voice, or the room. He wasn't sure if when the voice was talking to him if anyone could hear him answering or not, but he was sure that it was just held between the two of them.

After a time, about ten minutes, he thought that he was better. The tiny rest on the floor had made him feel like he could take it again. Fred was escorted into the room and chained to the floor. The attorney for the women was smiling at him, like he knew something that Fred didn't. Doubtful, he thought. Fred knew a great deal more than most people did.

More composed, he sat very still and decided that he'd watch the attorney's mouth. If it didn't move, he wasn't going to answer him. That, to Fred, was about the best plan that he'd come up with in a while. So as soon as everyone was set, the attorney asked him if he needed anything.

"No. No, I'm fine now. I've had a little rest and I'm ready to begin anew." The attorney nodded and turned his back. The question threw Fred off his good mood when he didn't have any idea if the attorney or the mystery voice had said it. "I'm sorry, could you repeat that?"

The man turned. He knew his name, but it would continue to slip from him. Like his words from his mouth. A voice said that his name was Cameron. Cam Henderson. Fred decided to keep his mouth shut and only answer questions that wouldn't be incriminating.

Not having any idea what he'd said so far, he figured that if he'd not been taken away, it had all been in his head. Fred was beginning to feel much better. But when Cam turned back to him, his hand holding onto Fred's stash, whatever was said to him then, Fred figured it wasn't going to help him at all.

~*~

Brody was having a wonderful time at the trial. He'd been called away once to his last patient at his offices, and had returned in time to hear what Fred had to say about the stash and why he had been mutilated at the clinic Fred had been taken to as a boy. Fred had even offered to show it to them, but no one said yes. Thankfully. Looking at the photos had been too much.

Brody had started his new job as police medical examiner today. There had been a lot of forms he'd had to fill out, nothing out of the ordinary; not for taking on the position that he was going to be doing.

The pay was less than he'd been making as a doctor, but that didn't bother him. When they needed him, Brody could still help out. And he could see a patient or two in his new place at the house. Not many, but he could should he want.

There was also a dress code, and that basically meant that he was armed and would wear a vest out in the field. He wasn't sure how he felt about carrying a gun, but he had one now. The theory of that was, if the killer was still out there, he could defend himself should it become necessary.

Brody was going to do the job of the coroner now as well. He'd been doing that anyway in the small towns that he'd been practicing in.

When the courtroom was called to order, he was curious about what was going to come up next. It surely had an entertainment value that he'd not expected.

Now they got to the good part of this man's crimes. Cam had been teasing Fred all morning by talking to him through a link, and then bombarding him with questions after he was so flustered that Fred was confused. He'd answered them all, and even told a few things that they'd not been expecting. Like the death of the cat. That had not only been something he'd not wanted to hear, but it was sort of sickening to think what that poor cat had suffered at his hands.

"Mr. Simmons, earlier you told us about a stash that you had. It took this courtroom several minutes to try and figure out what it was, but then you told us that you'd been collecting pubic hairs of your victims. Why is that?" Fred said nothing. "There were about fifty or so of them in the bag that had been sealed. And each one of the smaller bags, the ones with the actual hairs in them, have been dated and the woman's name they had come from put on them. Did you know that these names are the names of all the victims that have been in this room today? As a matter of fact, there are about a dozen of them that are on the list of missing persons. Did you kill them in the barn there?"

"I have nothing to say." Cam was on a roll, and Brody thought he was having a better time than he'd thought he might. Cam told Fred that he'd told them already, but just wanted him to be clearer on it. "I have nothing to say."

"It's a bit late for that, don't you think? I mean, not only did you tell us where to find your things you took from the bodies, but you also told us that you used the machinery out there to cut the bodies up to a more manageable size to put into the kiln." Cam waited a few seconds. "All right, if you don't wish to talk about that, then we'll talk about other things that you spoke of. You killed the doctor, the surgeon that did the operation that made you what you are today. And then there was the death of your mother. You said that you killed her by cutting her up with a chainsaw after escaping from the clinic that she sent you to. You told me and the courtroom that you'd enjoyed the sounds of her screams until she was dead. The doctor's body was found, but your mother's hasn't been. Can you tell us where you buried her?"

"I didn't bury her." Brody thought that he was going to say more, but all he did was look at Cam. "I haven't any idea what you're talking about anyway."

"Don't you, Mr. Simmons? Well, I hope that I can jog your memory when it comes to a couple of the women that you mentioned. You said that they touched you. I was wondering if you could elaborate on that a bit more. Touched you sexually?"

"No one touches me sexually, you moron. Didn't you see the pictures of what my mother had done to me?" Cam said he had. "Then you'd know for a fact that no one would look at me, much less touch me. They couldn't touch me because I

176

wasn't leaving any part of me behind. If I had anything to do with this mess you're talking about."

"That makes sense, I guess." Cam picked up another picture. "And is this the barn that you brought these women to when they dared to touch you? You did tell us about that, as I said earlier." Again, nothing from Fred. "You're making this very difficult, Mr. Simmons. Earlier you seemed to want to tell all, but now you're not saying a word."

"Yes, well, I haven't any idea what you might be talking about."

Cam nodded again, and Brody looked down at his phone when it vibrated.

*Don't look at the door when it opens, but just watch Fred's face.*

Jake, the presiding judge, had messaged that to him, and he looked at Fred. When the door opened, slamming hard against the walls, Brody was glad that he was looking directly at Fred or he might have missed it.

He paled to nearly a complete wash out. Fred stood, then sat three times before he whimpered. And when he looked at Jake then back at the door again, Brody had to wonder what or who was there. Then Cam said something about wind and doors, and walked back towards the door.

"No." Fred whimpered louder now, his entire body stiff with fear. Brody continued to watch him until the person that had come in was standing right in front of Fred. His face was still pale, but it was also tight with fear. "No. Go away. I don't want you here."

*It's his mother. She's come to haunt him for what he's done. I don't know how Wally managed it, but he found her and helped her come to see her son. Also, the dead women are lined up to see him next.*

Cam winked at him as he shut both of the doors and made his way to the front again. The room was not seeing the

177

ghost, just them and Fred. And when Ms. Simmons started to slip and slide over herself, the small pieces of her having a difficult time holding their shape, Fred screamed that this couldn't be happening, and begged for someone to make her go away.

"Her?" Cam walked around, looking around like he didn't see Ms. Simmons. "Who is here, Fred? I don't see anyone. Are you sure that you're — ?"

"It's my mother. She's standing right in front of me. Can't you see her? She's all in pieces, just like I cut her up to be." Then when another ghost, Brody didn't know their names, started to file into the room, Fred tried to get away, his body straining against the chains that held him there. "They're here. All of them are here. They're going to kill me."

"Who?" Cam nearly laughed when he asked this time, but he regained control just in time, Brody thought. "You'll have to be more specific Fred. I don't see anyone here."

Not only did he tell that he'd killed the women that were in the room with all of them, but how he'd done it. There were dates too that Fred started to spew forward, dates that Brody would bet corresponded with some of the dates on the little hairs.

Fred didn't stop talking even when asked to. He told of women that he'd popped in the mouth for getting smart with him. How he didn't get up for anyone if he rode public transit. He'd been late on a library book, but instead of paying the fine, he'd just slipped it back in the place and put it on the shelf. Small and large, Fred told them everything that they needed, and shit that they didn't. He was being dragged away, still confessing to everything from petty theft to grand larceny.

The courtroom was quiet after that. No one moved or said a word. There were people that had been taking notes on what was being said, and a couple of the bailiffs had to have a seat when they returned. It was by far the oddest and most informative trial Brody had been to. Then Jake spoke.

"Ladies and gentlemen, I'm not sure what to say." There was some small laughter. "As you know, everything said here today should not be repeated. Nor are you to go to the newspapers with this until such time as we can...I have no idea. Figure this out. We'll be solving cases for years, I think."

Another small laughter and Jake called it a day. People began filing out and Brody sat there, listening to what people had to say as they left the big room. Most of them were happy that families would get closure. Some were blown away that Fred had only done the things they'd heard. A lot of the people had always known, they said, that Fred was a terrible man.

When the doors closed behind them, they were locked. Cam gathered up his things and Brody just sat there. He and Emmi were the only two in the pews toward the back of the room, and he saw Cattie and Tyson in the front, coming from where Fred had been taken. They were talking quietly, but he could hear them well enough.

Fred was being taken to the hospital. He was going to be evaluated again, and then they'd decide where to go from there. The Feds could now clean up the mess they'd found out at the farm, what they were calling where the cars and such were. A lot of people would now know where their family member was, and that had been what Emmi had wanted all along.

Jake came to sit with him and Emmi. He looked like he'd been hung out to dry in the rain too, and said he felt that way when Emmi pointed it out. Tomorrow was going to be another long day, but for now, they were finished with what was happening.

"I have a favor to ask of you." Brody told Jake that he'd

do just about anything for him. "You're a good man. But this isn't much. I'd like for you to look over some things for us. As you know, we have been talking to the ghosts at Henry's house, and there are a couple of things that we don't know what we've found."

"Why do you think that I can help you?" He said he thought they were pieces of medical equipment from decades ago. "All right. I can do that. Anything else?"

"Yes, come by the house with the rest of the gang and hang out. We're not having pizza—we've had enough of that—but Forrest is coming home with about two hundred bucks' worth of Chinese food, and we're going to pig out. We might have to order pizzas later, but for now, we're going to eat really bad-for-us food and put today behind us." Brody said he could do that if Jordan and Aaron wanted to come. "They're already at the house getting the plates and other things ready."

A nice way to end the day, Brody thought. And he hadn't had any Chinese food for a while. He was reasonably sure that Jordan had never had it. His mother had hated the smell of it. This was going to be a good night, and he rode to Jake's house with him.

# Chapter 13

The body was still slightly warm, but Brody didn't remark on it. They were talking about the manner in which the woman had been killed, not how long ago. She'd been wrapped in a large area rug and dragged out to this secluded place along a road. Only the top of the rug was open enough to see her face and the area near her breasts. He'd not been able to open it much more, just to look where he could, until the photographer got there.

Touching his pen to the mark at her throat, he determined that it was the cut that had killed her. The other wounds were superficial and done after the death, he thought. That had confused him too, but he didn't have the entire body to work with just yet.

Brody didn't think that she had been killed the way it looked. The knife was sticking out of her head—her eye, as a matter of fact. It it wasn't the right length or the right style. Looking at it, he asked how much longer they'd have to wait on pictures to be taken, and was startled back on his ass when the ghost of the woman appeared before him.

No one with him could see her—he'd figured that out

a few weeks ago when he'd been working the field. Brody had been doing this job now for a month, and tomorrow was Thanksgiving. He wasn't going to hurry through this, but neither was he going to waste time if he didn't have to.

So, under the semblance of talking to himself, the way that he had explained it before, he started asking questions. Then when she answered him, if she knew the answer, he'd say it aloud for everyone to hear. They all must have thought him insane.

"This wasn't the knife that killed her, I don't think." The woman shook her head. She could speak if she remembered how, but nothing much more than that. He looked away when Wally appeared beside the woman. "No, not the knife that killed her. So why stab her with it after she was dead?"

"She said that the knife that he used is over yonder near the apple tree. Hard to tell what an apple tree is, but she's from these parts and knows all the trees here. I can read words now, too, about trees and such. That Christy, she—" Getting Wally to focus sometimes was a fulltime job. "Yeah, leaning against the apple tree. He must have forgotten it."

"Can you guys have a look around? For a knife that might be serrated on the tip, but would be fairly long?" In five minutes they'd found the knife. "All right, my dear, why were you killed? Domestic abuse? Did you do something that made someone angry with you?"

"She said that it was her husband. And she has a brother that she'd like for you to call for her. You can do that. You're not going to find information about him at her home." Brody nodded. "I'll tell you when we leave here."

"Good."

The photographer finally showed up and started taking pictures of the body and the rug. It was cheap and dirty, and might hold more clues if he could get her out of it soon. Then he asked if he could unwrap her from the rug when Johnny, the photo guy, went to take pictures of the knife.

Her purse was right on her chest where her breasts were. Handing it to the cops, he smiled when they said they'd been looking for it. Not so far as he'd seen. All they were doing was drinking coffee and talking.

"Good job, Doc. We've been looking."

Her name was Mary Bennett. Wally told him her brother's name was Easton Hunter. The cops behind him continued to speak, but not to him. He started to unwrap the rest of her body. She was heavier than he thought she looked, and he pulled the rug off her as the cops talked about the husband.

"Husband, I'm betting. I know Wendel Bennett. He'd beat his own mother if he could get by with it." That solved that part.

When she was finally free enough to get her out of the rug, Brody pulled it off her lower waist. What he found there not only scared him for how long she'd been there, but also about what he had to do now. Brody yelled for help.

The baby boy was tiny, but he'd not been hurt by the beating that took his mother's life. An ambulance was called for, and when it arrived, Brody had not only given the baby a good bill of health, but had also taken a sample of his blood, as well as that of his mother. In no time the child was on his way to get cleaned up, and Brody's crime scene took on another aspect altogether.

The husband had tried to kill both the mother and child, and that would be murder as well as attempted murder to add to his list of crimes. Brody finished up now that he had examined her entire body, and he sent her to the hospital for more tests. Tests on her body would tell who her child belonged to, and perhaps how long she might have been in labor before she was killed.

183

After he was finished cleaning up, Brody told the police all he could figure out. Some that the woman had told him too. When Wally talked to Mary, she'd told him what had happened up to her death.

"I believe that she was in labor and wanted her husband to more than likely take her to the hospital. I would guess that something happened that pissed him off. I don't know, perhaps he didn't want to be bothered and wanted her to drive herself. Which, as you know, would have been dangerous to them all." Conley, one of the police officers, asked Brody if the rug was from their home. "I would say so, yes. I mean, she wasn't killed here, so that would be my guess."

It was her rug and she had been killed at home. Mary told him through Wally that she didn't have anything for the child either. Her husband had drank it all up when he found her stash of money from when her mom had passed away.

"Are you going to contact her brother?" Conley said that Cattie was going to do it for them. "She'll be good at it. Very compassionate."

Driving himself to the hospital, Wally and Mary rode with him. She was still talking through Wally, but he could hear her too. When she mentioned that she had another child at home, he called out to Cattie to let her know.

*I'm headed to the house now. How old is the child?* Mary told him that her daughter was six, but she was very backward and terrified of men. *I'll take care that the men with me stay away. Does she know where her husband might be? That would help me a great deal if I know that he's not there.*

*She said that he's more than likely at the bar at the other end of town.* Cattie said she'd send someone there to pick him up. *He cut her throat, Cattie. That takes a strong, sick man to be able to look someone in the eye and kill them. Especially his very pregnant wife.*

*I'll have him in a cell before he can do much of anything to my*

184

*men. I warned them that he's to be considered armed and dangerous. We're at the home now, Brody. And it looks bad.* He didn't know what that meant, but figured that Cattie wouldn't exaggerate on this one. *I'm entering with my men. I'm not going to take a chance that the house will fall down on me while inside. Also, there is no heat that I can detect, nor any running water. Christ.*

It took her ten minutes to get back to him. And then all she said was that she had the child. It must have been bad too, because he could hear the anger in her voice. Tyson told him to wait in the ER, that Cattie wanted him to have a look at the child. All Brody asked was, is the little girl still alive.

*No.*

The finality of that single word broke his heart. Six. No older than his own son. And when the cruiser came in the ER parking lot, he was waiting for her when Cattie came in.

The child was wrapped in a blanket and nothing more. The blood seeping through it had saturated not just it, but Catties uniform as well. She said that she'd brought the child in because the house had been so very cold, and that she didn't want evidence on this one to go unchecked.

Brody took the small bundle to the closed off room and pulled the blanket away. He wanted to cry. Brody wanted to find the man responsible for this and kill him in much the same way he had his wife and child. When Mary appeared this time, she had her daughter with her and she looked happy. Brody thought that she would be, knowing that her daughter was with her, but all he could think about was a life cut so terribly short. Cattie joined him in the room with a photographer and a recording device.

"I'd like for you to tell me the cause of death, Dr. Downs. And give me an estimate on how long she's been deceased." He nodded at Cattie, while she tried her best and failed at remaining professional and not crying. "She's so tiny, isn't she?"

"Yes. For a six-year-old, I'd say that she's about twenty pounds underweight, as well as short in stature." He asked Cattie where she'd been. "That would explain it if she'd spent a great deal of her little life in a cage. There are marks here that tell me she was also chained up, and since she's still wearing a diaper, I'd say that her mental capacity was stunted."

He said that while he couldn't give her a good time of death, what with her being nearly frozen through, he'd say she'd been gone about six or seven hours. About the same time for the mother. Then he told her the cause of death.

"Starvation, with a secondary cause being excessive blood loss. Her being so weak, it would have made her death quicker. She must have tried to claw her way out or something, and cut herself up badly. I don't know for sure, but I'd give that my best bet."

Mary and her daughter came to stand next to him and Cattie. The little girl didn't speak, but the mother could now.

"I found her this morning before I went into labor. I was going to get to the hospital and tell them what Wendel had done to her, putting her in that cage and all." Cattie asked Mary if she had tried to get help. "We got no phone out there, and the heat and water has been off for about three months. It was okay when it was warmer, but it's been too cold for much since the weather changed."

"I'm so sorry." Mary nodded and looked at the body of her daughter, then over at her own body. "Your son, he's doing well. Did you want to see him?"

"I can't go to him. He might see me, and I don't want him to see his momma like this. Will you call my brother? He can take care of him for me. When he finds out about what Wendel did to us, he's going to come running." Cattie told her that she'd do it as soon as she left there. "He's a good man,

Easton. Wendel, he never liked him because he is gay. But I never cared. He was my only brother, and I loved him all to pieces."

"I have a brother who's gay. We're twins." Mary said that her and Easton were just like normal. "Is there anything that I can tell him for you, Mary? You know the rules, but I can tell him anything about how you thought of him."

"I did think of him all the time. I had his number with me when I was killed. I was going to go to him. I don't know how. Wendel took all my money. I didn't even have a single diaper for my little man." She didn't cry, but they could tell that she was heartbroken. "You tell Easton that I thought of him all the time. And that we was coming to see him. We didn't get to, but I still love him more than anyone in the world but my kids."

"I'll tell him that." Mary started to fade away, then came back. Brody could only imagine what this hanging around was costing her. Mary told her the name that she wanted the baby to be called if Easton had a mind to. "Alexander Patch Hunter. I'll tell him for you."

Then she was gone, taking her daughter with her. Brody knew that she'd be around, and that he could call on her if he wished. But he was going to try very hard to let her have peace now. And see that her little boy got the best of care.

Going home that night, he held Jordan for a long time, well after he'd fallen asleep. And when he put him to bed, Aaron helped him tuck Jordan in. He had told his lover what had happened, and it tore them both up to know that someone had done that to a child. To starve — it would have taken a long time for the little girl to surrender to death like that. And her desperation to have tried so hard to get out to eat something, anything, would have taken all she had left.

~*~

187

Easton sat in his living room and sobbed. His sister was dead, and so was Peaches. His niece hadn't had a good life, no more so than Mary had. Easton had called her daughter Peaches since the first time he'd seen her. And it was also the last.

Getting up to make arrangements to go to them, he thought about all the things that he wanted to do to Wendel. The fucking bastard was going to pay, and when Easton caught up with him, he was going to make him suffer. But for now, he had to think about the child, the little baby. It had only survived because his mom had been killed and someone had found her in time.

Packing up his clothing, he made a mental note of the things he was going to have to take care of. Funeral arrangements would have to be made for Mary and Peaches. Then there would be the house that he would have to clean out, as well as seeing about getting Alex some things to come home with him in. There was nothing, the police officer had told him. No bed, no clothing, not even a bottle to take care of Alex when he came home. If he came home.

"She was coming to you, we think. Your number was clutched in her hand when her body was found. I don't know for sure, but I'd say it was a safe bet." Easton thanked the cop. "I'm so sorry, sir. I truly am. But we're looking for Wendel now, and we'll have him in custody well before you arrive."

He didn't want her to find him. Easton wanted that pleasure for himself. While he had no idea how either of them had died, he had a feeling that it hadn't been fast, nor without a great deal of pain. Mary had suffered much in her lifetime. More than she should have, he thought.

Taking the first flight out of New York, Easton thought of his lover Todd. He'd been killed a week ago by a bunch of homophobes. They had murdered him, then left his body out

188

in the cold weather under a snowbank, hoping, he supposed, that he'd never be found. But he could and did find him, because Todd had changed him to a wolf several months ago. He had found him only hours after he'd been shot once in the head.

Now, he was alone. And more alone than he'd thought just hours ago. His sister and her family were gone as well. Easton had no idea what he was going to have to do to be able to press on. There was little to nothing left in his life that mattered, he thought.

Todd hadn't been his mate. They were just two lonely gay men that had hooked up several years ago. Todd had lost his mate long ago, and wanted companionship. Easton hadn't found anyone that he wanted to spend more than ten minutes with until Todd had come along.

The trip was short and uneventful. By the time he had gotten him a car and driven to the little town where his sister had lived, it was too late to do much. So, taking a hotel room, Easton settled in after telling Cattie that he was there.

Easton thought about going to see the baby, but he didn't want that right now. He would take care of him if he could figure it out, but he wasn't sure that he could raise him. Easton knew less about children and babies than most people knew about how to program a computer. And Easton had built a great many computers before he started designing games for different systems.

It was nearing midnight when he got up and decided to go to the hospital. It was about an hour from where he was, so he worked out his list for the morning. Easton knew that he wasn't going to get any sleep for a few days anyway.

His cell was ringing when he pulled into the hospital parking lot.

"I thought you'd still be awake. We've got Wendel in

189

custody, and he's not talking, for which I'm glad. I don't think I want to hear his excuses for what he did." Easton asked Cattie what the cause of death had been for Mary. "He slit her throat, then wrapped her up in a rug. He dumped her about forty minutes from where he was living with her."

"And my niece. I'm sorry, but I only met her the one time, and she was just a baby. I have always called her Peaches." She told him that her name had been Margaret. "Margaret. What was her cause of death?"

He wasn't sure she was going to tell him, and that made his imagination run wild. When she finally told him, Easton laid his head on the steering wheel and cried. Starvation. Bleeding out. What a way for a little girl to have met with her death. When he had better control of his emotions, he asked her what else she could tell him.

"Margaret had been caged like an animal, we found out. Mary was getting food help for a while, but she stopped coming in to apply and that soon ran out too. Knowing her husband, with what I'm finding out about him, he more than likely didn't take her to sign up or something." Easton said that sounded like something he'd do. "She had a garden, we saw, and there were frozen things in the freezer. There was no heat in the house, nor running water. Wendel would go into town and take a bath at the homeless shelter every once in a while. I think that's why no one knew that he had a family. It would be just him. And so far, I'm not finding anyone that had seen Mary during her pregnancy with either child."

"My sister, she would have tried to take care of them. I don't think she would have let Margaret go without food, even if she had to take some of her own to give it to her." Cattie told him that she had no idea, as no one had known about her. "I should have come home more often. It would cost me, not in money, but in dignity to see her. But it was

190

never at the house or any place where Wendel would find us. He didn't think that me being a homo, his words, would have been tolerable to him. So we'd sneak around and hide from him. I think the last time I was there was when Peaches was born. Five or six years ago."

"She was six. A friend of mine is doing the autopsies tomorrow. And I'll be there with him. He'll have a better picture of what might have been going on long term with that. Wendel, as I said, isn't talking, but we're finding out a great deal about him regardless." Easton told her that he was going to see the baby. "You'll meet Brody. He's the doctor that delivered Alex and figured out what we know now."

Going into the hospital and finding the nursery, someone must have left word for him to be shown up, as the hours for visiting had long since passed. Dr. Downs met him at the elevator when it opened.

Almost as soon as he shook hands with the man, he felt a comfort that he'd not had since Todd had been killed. And when the bigger man pulled him in for a hug, Easton fell apart. Before he could gather himself, he was taken to an empty room and held. It was just what he needed, someone to help him with his grief.

After he was able to gather himself, Easton told Brody, as he was asked to call him, that he wanted to see the baby. He was gowned up and taken to a private room where the cradle-like thing was placed. The nurse was dismissed, and Brody handed little Alex to him. Easton fell in love at first sight.

"From some of the tests I've been able to run on him, I'd say he's about three weeks early. Trauma brought his labor on, I'm guessing, and we were lucky to have been there when he came into the world. Otherwise he might have frozen to death." Easton was handed the tiniest bottle he'd ever seen

191

to feed Alex with. Brody continued talking, telling him things that he might need to know. "He weighs a little under seven pounds, which is a good weight for him. And he's in good health, considering that Mary hadn't had any care during her pregnancy."

"I don't know what I'm going to do now." Brody said that he hadn't thought he would—it had been very quick with everything going on all the way around. "I'm going to hang around for a few days, to see to things for my sister's family. I'm going to have to find me a place to stay, however. The hotel where I'm staying is booked up for the holiday, and they were only able to get me one night."

"You'll come stay with me. And before you even think to tell me no, where would you live if not for my home? The house is plenty big enough for you and anyone else." Easton thanked him. "And, because you will be staying, you will of course have dinner with us. Everyone will be there for Thanksgiving dinner."

"Thanksgiving. I completely forgot about that. I don't want to put you out." Brody assured him that he wouldn't. They were catering it. "Good for you. All right. But only because I've literally nowhere else to go."

When Alex had drank his bottle, Easton held him for a little while longer. He was so tiny, he thought, and could see traces of his sister in his little face. Easton decided right then that he'd raise Alex as his own, even if he had to hire a bevy of housekeepers.

"And I'll tell you about your mom all the time. Your sister too." Easton wondered if he could get some pictures, if there were any, and decided that what he didn't know, he'd make up. Just so the boy would have a better picture of his family than Easton knew of. "I love you Alex. Very much."

## Before You Go...

# HELP AN AUTHOR

## *write a review*

# THANK YOU!

Share your voice and help guide other readers to these wonderful books. Even if it's only a line or two your reviews help readers discover the author's books so they can continue creating stories that you'll love. Login to your favorite retailer and leave a review. Thank you.

AWARD WINNING, BESTSELLING AUTHOR

Kathi Barton, winner of the Pinnacle Book Achievement award as well as a best-selling author on Amazon and All Romance books, lives in Nashport, Ohio with her husband Paul. When not creating new worlds and romance, Kathi and her husband enjoy camping and going to auctions. She can also be seen at county fairs with her husband who is an artist and potter.

Her muse, a cross between Jimmy Stewart and Hugh Jackman, brings her stories to life for her readers in a way that has them coming back time and again for more. Her favorite genre is paranormal romance with a great deal of spice. You can visit Kathi online and drop her an email if you'd like. She loves hearing from her fans. aaronskiss@gmail.com.

Follow Kathi on her blog: http://kathisbartonauthor. blogspot.com/

www.ingramcontent.com/pod-product-compliance
Lightning Source LLC
Chambersburg PA
CBHW030223180626
46810CB00008B/2938